MISSING

NEVER LOST

BECA LEWIS

PERCEPTION PUBLISHING

CONTENTS

*N*othing *dreamed is ever lost, and nothing lost forever.*
—Joanne Harris, Runelight

Nothing is ever truly lost
The world is like the tide
Returning, for an instant, to the place it occupied before
Or leaving that same place once more
Celebrate, then, for what you lose shall be returned
Smile, then, for all good deeds you do shall be visited upon you
Weep, then, for all ills you do shall return to you
Or your children, or your children's children
What is reaped is what is sown.
What is sown is what is reaped. — Robert Jackson Bennett

When I despair, I remember that all through history, the way of truth and love has always won. There have been murderers and tyrants, and for a time they can seem invincible. But in the end they always fall. Think of it, always. —Mohandas Karamchand Gandhi

ONE

S he opened her eyes. She saw stars—real ones swimming among the branches of the trees high above her. No moon. At least not where she could see it.

She thought she should move. Perhaps sit up or rollover, but she was afraid.

What she was afraid of she didn't know, which was the problem. She didn't know. Anything.

At least about herself. All she knew for sure was that she was in the woods and that there were stars in the sky.

But that didn't begin to fill the entire empty space she found in her head. All the essential things to know were gone. Disappeared. Missing.

Where was she? Who was she?

She thought that perhaps if she shut her eyes and opened them again, she would know. So she tried that. More than once. But each time, it was the same.

She was nobody, somewhere.

She wondered if she had ever been this frightened before. She didn't know that any more than she knew anything else.

Was she afraid because she couldn't remember, or was she afraid for another reason?

As she lay there, the sky lightened, and she did know one thing. She was hungry.

Eventually, she would need to eat. She would need to get out of the sleeping bag and stop hiding.

Perhaps if she got up, she would remember.

A surge of hope helped her sit up. Nothing. She was not even dizzy.

If something happened to me, wouldn't I feel something, she wondered to herself. Almost said it out loud, and then did, thinking maybe that would trigger a memory.

She whispered the question, "Who am I?" No one answered.

Sighing, she unzipped her sleeping bag and looked around and then down at herself.

What she saw didn't spark a memory. So she noted what she saw, cataloging it as if she was studying someone else.

Without seeing a mirror, she guessed she was young, maybe around twenty. Thin, but probably athletic because she could see muscles in her legs. A pair of hiking boots beside what was a dying fire told her she hiked. Looking around, she saw a backpack hanging in the trees. To keep animals out of it. She knew that much. It was something.

Quickly slipping on her boots, she retrieved the backpack and dumped it onto the sleeping bag, looking for an answer to the question of who she was. Once she remembered that, everything else would fall into place. She was sure of that.

Food bars, a water bladder, a change of clothes, a few pairs of socks, plus sunglasses and sunscreen. Nothing that told her anything that helped her remember how she came to be in the woods.

Just a name, she sobbed. Tell me my name.

Scattering everything and emptying all the pockets in the pack revealed nothing, so she stuffed everything back in, grabbed a food bar and water, and slid back into the sleeping bag. She would go back to sleep. And wake up again.

Maybe this was only a dream. When she woke up, she would remember.

She took a bite of the bar, a swig of the water, and pulled the bag up over her head.

That's when she discovered something else about herself. When she was afraid, she hid.

Somehow she fell asleep. Perhaps the sheer panic she felt had exhausted her. The sun was slanting through the trees when she woke up again. For a moment, she thought she remembered who she was, but then realized that what she remembered was only what had happened the last time she had woken up.

Trying to find hope somewhere, she was grateful that at least she wasn't having a groundhog day moment. She didn't have to repeat something over and over again. She just had no memory of who she was, where she had come from, or why she was there.

Sitting back on her heels, she started laughing. She was brand new. She could be anyone—at least until she remembered who she was before today.

Not everyone got a chance to be brand new. That's what she told herself to get herself out of the sleeping bag.

It was time to start walking because food bars would not last her long. She didn't know how far away civilization was. It could be just past the trees, or it could be miles away.

As she rolled up her bag, she felt a lump at the bottom. Fishing inside, she pulled out a pair of pants and a jacket.

Ah, she thought, I am smart too. I was keeping these warm and safe at the bottom of my bag. Which was when she realized she might have put the crucial things in the sleeping bag with her instead of in the backpack. The pants and the jacket had pockets. Lots of pockets. She reached into all of them and pulled out everything.

Leaving the mess on the bag, she slipped the pants over her tights and the jacket over the t-shirt to keep herself from shivering in the morning air, then she stared at what she had uncovered.

A few knives and a can of spray. Smart, she said again to herself. A rubber band held a wad of money together. At least she could eat. She unfolded the money, expecting that there she would find her driver's license or something that told her who she was. But there was nothing.

Now she had a choice. Start crying or start walking. Or both. Cry and walk, which is exactly what she decided to do.

An hour later, following the faintest of trails, she had a thought: If I hide when I am afraid, and yet I am smart and prepared, perhaps I forgot who I am on purpose.

No, she added to herself. That would be stupid. Then I wouldn't know who or what I am hiding from—if that's what I'm doing. Maybe I don't have any identification, so no one could find me. No one would ever plan on waking up one day with no knowledge about themselves.

So, no. Not on purpose, she decided. *But now that I can reinvent myself, I will. At least for now. And I will hide because that seems like the smart thing to do.*

TWO

She tried not to overthink while she walked. When she found walking poles beside the sleeping bag, she had smiled. At least she knew that hiking was something she knew how to do.

Perhaps if she didn't worry, instinct would kick in and lead her to answers. If not answers, at least a town where she could eat something other than food bars.

One thing she kept doing was glancing at her wrist as if from habit. She must have worn a watch or tracker of some kind. Now she didn't have one. Or a phone. Both those things confirmed she was hiding. From who or what she didn't know, which meant she would have to be careful about showing herself or asking too many questions.

The hat she had found in the backpack had a huge brim in front, shading her entire face. Another sign that she didn't want to be seen.

Or, she thought, *to keep the sun off my face. Or both. Both,* she decided.

After an hour or two, the rhythm of walking kicked in, and despite the fear and anxiety, she started to relax and enjoy herself. Her body enjoyed walking. Although she couldn't remember the names of the trees or the plants she saw, she knew them anyway.

They felt like friends. The trail she was following was leading her towards the rising sun. East. She knew that much. She hoped that was where she intended to go.

She stopped every few hours. Sometimes to eat and drink, and once to change her socks.

Instinct, she told herself. She had done this countless times before. She must have known where she was going, and since there wasn't much food in her bag, she must have known there was a place to get more.

The more she thought about it, the more she realized she had planned whatever she was doing well. She knew how to hike and how to hide. If she had no technology on purpose, how did she know where she was going?

There had to be a map—somewhere. Maybe she missed it? She started patting her pockets and then thought of her hat. Talking it off, she felt around the inside band and found what she was looking for—a folded piece of paper with an address.

But that didn't help much. She still didn't know where she was. It was just an address with no name. How did that help? Why keep that? Was she afraid she'd forget it?

Although she still didn't know where she was or why she would go to that address, she would have to trust that was what she meant to do. And that heading east was the right direction to get to someplace called Doveland, Pennsylvania.

What was she supposed to do once she got there? Was she meeting someone there who could help her? Help her with what?

At least I have some idea of what to do next, she thought. *And since it seems I am hiding from someone or something, I'll accept that I am doing all this for a reason.*

In the first town she came to, she would get more information about how to get to that place called Doveland. And if she hadn't remembered her name yet, she would make one up and use it while she traveled.

On the way, perhaps her missing memory would return. And if not, maybe whoever was at the address would know her.

· · · ● · ● · ● · · ·

Ace Tillman was frantic. He had lost her. How? He had done everything right. But obviously, she hadn't fallen for it. She had fooled him. She had acted as if she loved him. Maybe she never had. Perhaps she had known all along who he was and what he intended to do.

No matter what, he needed to find her before Leo found out she was missing. It had been two days since she left. He had told Leo that she had gone hiking and would be back soon.

That part was true. He knew she was walking. She did that all the time. It was something he admired about her from the beginning. He had gone walking with her a few times, but it was so boring he stopped. Boring and hard.

Ace preferred his kind of work. When he first came home, that was what he thought had happened. She had gone for a hike. She often did that on a whim. She always left a note on the kitchen counter telling him where she was and when she would be back.

She had done that this time too. Said she would be back in the morning. But she hadn't come back, and now, two days had gone by without hearing from her. Either she had met with an accident—his heart ceased at that possibility—or she was gone on purpose.

After he realized that her computer was missing, Ace started to worry. He planned to look at her searches and emails. She never took her laptop on a hike. She must have taken it away or hid it somewhere in the apartment so he wouldn't know where she had gone. That's when he had suspected that she had known all along.

Panicked, he searched everywhere. It wasn't there. Other than a missing computer, everything was as it always was. Neat and tidy. Clean.

It was something they always argued about. He made messes, and she made him clean them up. Not at first. At first, she had smiled and picked up the dishes and clothes as if that was part of her job. He didn't make her do it.

"I just can't stand messes," she would say to him.

But eventually, she tired of picking up after him and became such a bitch about it, he couldn't stand it. She nagged and nagged at him to pick up after himself. He did. But only because Leo said to do it to keep the peace.

But even though Ace did what he considered a decent job of it, he could tell it still annoyed her. It wasn't good enough. *Nothing was good enough for her,* Ace mumbled under his breath.

Not that she didn't try to hide her annoyance. But it was like a smell in the air. Ace thought she had hidden her irritation with him because she loved him, but now that he thought about it, maybe it was because she had a reason to stay with him too.

Sitting on the couch, peeling the label off the beer he was drinking, he felt like throwing the bottle at the wall. He only refrained because he didn't need the nosy neighbors calling the police. They'd been there before. It wouldn't look good if they came again, and she was missing.

She was already in deep trouble if he found her, but if he discovered that she had been playing him all along, well, that deserved a different kind of punishment. After Leo got what he wanted, of course, then she would be all his. But first, he had to find her.

Although he had installed a tracker on her phone and her car, both of them were off. That was another reason he knew she had run. Well, not run. Walked. All her hiking gear was gone. She meant to throw him off for a few days.

Well, it worked. He had wasted days. Now he had to figure out where she went and go after her. She thought she was smart, but she was not as smart as he was.

THREE

It was almost nightfall before she came to a road. She debated whether she should camp by the side of the road or keep walking, and decided to keep walking.

An hour later, just as the stars started showing in the sky, she found a motel. A vacancy sign swung on rusted chains creaking in the wind. That the motel looked as if it would crumble into the ground didn't deter her. It was a place to stop. And they probably wouldn't mind if she just showed up and paid cash. This was not a place that needed to know her name. She'd make one up if they asked.

But they didn't. The woman at the counter barely looked at her. "Fifty bucks," the woman barked, a cigarette hanging off her lip. It wasn't lit.

Grateful for small blessings, she reached inside her jacket pocket and produced two twenties and a ten. She had stopped outside the ring of lights around the parking lot to prepare, not wanting to show how much money she had with her. Even if she wasn't hiding, she wasn't that stupid.

The room was as bad as she thought it would be. She had no intention of sleeping on the bed, but the floor was even worse, so she peeled back the bedspread and top sheet and put the bag on top of that. She would have taken the bottom sheet off but was afraid to see the mattress.

What she wanted was a shower. Then some real food. She had seen a small pizza place on the other side of the motel. It was hard to mess up pizza. The shower pressure was low, but the water was hot.

Using the small bag of toiletries she found in her backpack, she washed her hair, feeling the short strands. They didn't feel familiar. She probably had cut her hair somewhere along the way.

She hadn't looked in the mirror yet, avoiding it as she stripped off her clothes and washed them with her in the shower, including the socks she had worn that day. If they weren't dry in the morning, she would hand dry them with the blow dryer attached to the wall, obviously meant to keep people from stealing it, but a good yank would have done it.

Finally, she could put it off no longer. She used the towel to wipe away the steam on the mirror and looked at the face in the mirror, hoping she would know it.

She didn't.

• • • ● • ● • • ·

The pizza place wasn't as bad as the motel. And it definitely smelled better. Not remembering what kind of pizza she liked, she ordered a supreme.

Yes, she would eat it there, she answered the teenager behind the counter, figuring that she could eat cold pizza for breakfast and lunch the next day. She also ordered a diet Dr. Pepper. Who knew why? It sounded good. Taking the cup he handed her, she filled it while glancing around the shop. Nothing told her where she was or when she was.

"What's the closest town," she asked the boy.

"Doesn't matter," he answered. "Not much there."

When she didn't move, he added, "Where are you heading?"

For a moment she started to say Doveland, Pennsylvania, but then stopped herself and shrugged.

"On a walkabout?" he asked.

"Something like that," she answered, wondering how this boy knew about walkabouts.

"Have you been on one yourself?"

"Oh, yeah. Just short ones, though. Someday I am moving to a city and becoming somebody. Even if I have to walk there."

"I understand that," she replied, and for some reason, she did.

"Pizza will be ready in a few," he said and turned his attention back to the TV.

"What's that you're watching?"

"A rerun of Ru Paul's Drag race season eleven final."

When she gave him a puzzled look, he added, "You know, drag queens. It's amazing theater. I knew these two would end up competing at the end. They are so good. He pointed to the two performers. That one is Brooke Lynne, and the other is Yvie Oddly. They are amazing. It's doesn't matter who wins. They make each other better."

She watched the boy watch the show. He had come alive.

"What do you like about this?"

"These guys are so courageous. And talented. The whole idea is you should be who you want to be and not let people's opinions stop you. That's what I like. You know what I mean?"

"I do," she said. And meant it.

Afterward, as she lay in her sleeping bag, she reviewed what the boy had said. She needed courage, and she needed to be who she was. If that meant she would remake herself, that is what she would do. And she would name herself after those two drag queens. She would be Evie Lynne.

For now, she would make up a story. Maybe it would be true, or at least parts of it. She was on a walkabout. She was heading for Pennsylvania. How long she had been walking, or where she came from, she didn't know.

But now she would say she was from here because that was where she was newly born. Pizza, a teenager, and RuPaul had given her new hope. If, along the way, she remembered who she used to be, she could go back to that, or not. Maybe the person she was choosing to be now would be someone she liked better.

She reached out to the light by the bed, trying not to touch anything but the switch, turned it off, and buried herself deep inside the sleeping bag. Tomorrow she would go to town and get more supplies, maybe wash the bag and clothes at a Laundromat, and head back on the trail.

"Good night, Evie," she said to herself. "Sweet dreams," she answered herself, closed her eyes, and slept the sleep of the dead.

FOUR

Thomas Hendrick walked through his living room, muttering to himself. What a mess. But he couldn't blame anyone. It was his mess.

His books were scattered everywhere, his shoes by the couch, his dirty dishes from last night that he never took into the kitchen were on the coffee table. Even if he had cleared them, that wouldn't have mattered. There were still dishes from three days ago stacked up on the counter.

Only when he ran out of clean dishes would he bother to wash them. Or else he would resort to using paper plates, which is why he no longer bought them. It was one way to force himself to clean up.

He muttered, *it's disgusting*, to himself every morning after stumbling out of bed, holding on to a cup of coffee he often resorted to brewing in a dirty cup.

He kept waiting for the day that he was so disgusted with himself that he did something about it. He was waiting for the day when he stopped wandering around all day wearing tattered sweatpants and an old t-shirt.

What was worse is they weren't the same ones every day. No, he had so many of them he could choose from a pile. When he used up that pile, he would move to the pile on the floor by the washing machine, wash them, and then start again.

Sometimes he bothered to shave. Sometimes he didn't. Mostly he didn't. Mutter and drink coffee, watch The View and mutter, and eat lunch. Mutter and watch more TV. Go to bed. Get up in the morning, pull another pair of sweatpants and T-shirt, and repeat exactly what he did the day before.

Before anyone else was up in the neighborhood, he would shuffle to the mailbox, bring the mail in, drop it into the basket by the door. Unopened. He'd get around to it, he would mutter. It had been weeks since he had last looked.

At least the tiny front lawn was mowed. But not by him. A local landscaper came by and mowed and tidied up. He collected his money from the envelope under the rock by the door. They never saw each other, just as Thomas wanted it.

Food was easy too. Everyone delivered. It was a brand new world. One he liked. It meant he didn't have to take part in or notice the world. Instead, he muttered, ate, and slept.

He was waiting to feel like himself again. But it had been so long since he had, he didn't know if he could ever return.

Thomas figured that one day he would die. And the only way people would know was there wouldn't be money under the stone. The landscaping guy would ring the doorbell. When Thomas didn't answer, maybe he would give up and go away and stop taking care of the yard.

The yard would soon be overrun with weeds, the grass would get too high, and the neighbors would complain. Perhaps they would ring the doorbell and smell something bad coming from the house. They would call the police. They would come and take him away.

After that, they would try to find someone who cared. They would fail.

And that was the crux of the problem. No one cared. So why should he? His daughter had been gone so long he figured she died.

When he retired, he thought people would remember him, that they would call him back so he could share the knowledge that he had accumulated for all these years. They didn't.

They moved on. Everyone had moved on without him. There was no one left who cared.

He had read about Native Americans knowing when their time was up going into the woods and waiting to die. He hadn't gone into the woods. He had gone into his house, shut the door, turned off the phone, and waited to die.

Years ago. Thomas waited, but he was still alive. He couldn't bring himself to end it on purpose. Thomas wanted it to be something that happened to him, not something he made happen. He was tired of making things happen. What good did it do? It never turned out the way anyone planned anyway. Certainly not for him.

As a young man, he had envisioned a bright future. But along the way the sun had set, and nothing had happened. Except he owned a home and had enough money for food. Death would be welcome. And yet he lived. This is what he muttered as he walked through his living room, "Why am I still alive?"

Every day he asked that question and got no answer. He knew that today would be no different.

Except something was. At 10:00 a.m. the doorbell rang. It had been so long since Thomas had heard the ring, he didn't recognize what it was until it rang again.

Geez, he said to himself, standing in the kitchen, *and I am not even dead yet. Or maybe I am, and I don't know it.*

He looked back into the living room and didn't see a dead body, so he figured he was still alive.

"Humph, now what," he muttered.

He was torn between ignoring the bell and answering the door.- Finally, curiosity won out and he shuffled over to the door, his big toe sticking out of his slipper, and cautiously opened it.

During the shuffling, it had occurred to him that it might be a Jehovah's witness at the door, and he didn't want that on his doorstep. If it was them, he was going to yell, "Get out."

Instead, it was the postman. He knew who it was. He had watched him for years delivering the mail. But this time he was standing there holding an envelope.

"Sorry, sir," the postman said. "But you have to sign for this."

Thomas stuck a hand out the door, grabbed the slip of paper and pen, scribbled his name, and handed it back.

Realizing he had been rude, he muttered, "Thank you," as the mailman handed him the envelope and walked away, shaking his head as if he was wondering how someone could be that private they could only show an eye and a hand to the postman.

Breathing hard, Thomas shut the door and leaned up against it. Yes, it was addressed to him, Thomas Hendrick. But he didn't recognize the name or the address of the person who sent it to him. This was a letter he would have to open.

"Best to sit down," he muttered to himself and shuffled over to the couch where he sat in the spot where he always sat. The indent was so deep that even if he sat in a different place, he would have slid into that spot anyway.

His hands shook as he struggled to open the letter. Finally, he grabbed the knife from last night's dinner and used it to slit it open.

The words swam in front of him. He leaned back onto the couch cushion, breathing even more heavily. He stopped breathing. He breathed again. He read the letter again. Was this a hoax?

Repeatedly closing and opening his eyes didn't make the words go away.

Everything had changed. Finally, this is how he found out something he had only hoped would be true. The impossible had become possible.

He had a granddaughter, and she was headed his way.

FIVE

S till, he sat. Never in his life had the impossible become
possible. Why now? Why did his granddaughter, the one he
didn't know he had, decide to come to him? The letter had been
so brief he could have written it.

Humph, he muttered to himself again. *Maybe it was true. She
inherited my brevity and clarity.*

That thought made him laugh. It had been so long since he had
laughed that it came out more like a frog hiccuping. But there it
was, laughter after all these years. He laughed because he looked
around at his life, and there was no clarity anywhere.

He muttered. He could barely understand himself let alone
communicate with clarity with someone else. His house was full
of junk. He had been sitting so long he resembled a squashed
mushroom. Well, the one thing he had been clear about was that
nothing mattered anymore.

It started the day his wife died. It confused him. *Why? What
kind of god gave him a daughter and took a wife?*

The more he asked himself that question, the more confused he
got about life, but still, he had loved his daughter with all his heart
and done everything he could for her. And then she left him.

How was that fair? Yes, since Ann died, clarity about life had escaped him.

But at work, he had been clear. He loved trying to solve the puzzles he encountered every day on the job. He had clarity in the search.

Thomas had also been clear about working to have money to buy his daughter clothes and books. He worked and saved money to buy this house. He had worked for the pension that now supported him. That was clear.

But everything about how he could lose the two people he loved more than life itself was as muddy as the creek that ran behind his house headed for the lake a few miles away.

He and Ann loved that lake, and their daughter, Maggie, had loved that lake too. They had picnics there on Saturdays because that was the best day for picnics.

He had been clear about doing everything for and with Maggie until she became clear about wanting to do things other than hang out with a boring father at the lake. He knew she kept going to the lake long after they stopped going together. He never went again.

Hadn't he read that they found bodies in that lake, buried deep in the mud? Mud that probably came from the creek behind his house. He had come to believe that nothing he ever did had clarity. He had been living in mud all along and hadn't known it.

And now this girl-woman was on her way to see him.

Why? When would she arrive? What about her mother, his daughter, Maggie? Where was she?

What his granddaughter had written answered none of these questions. Whatever had made him think she was clear? Brief, yes. Clear no. Although she said she would answer all his questions when she got there.

Thomas glanced at the envelope. It was postmarked four days before.

That took a long time to get here, he thought. *She could be right around the corner by now. It didn't take that long to get to Doveland from Oregon, did it?*

All it said was she was his granddaughter, she was looking forward to meeting him, and she needed his help. That was it. All other relevant information was missing. She did sign her name. Alice Gibbons.

How did she get that name? Did Maggie get married? To whom? Where had they been all this time?

He had so many questions and no answers.

What Thomas knew was that he couldn't let her meet him the way he was, the way he had allowed himself to become. It was time to return to life. Thomas looked across the room to where the pictures of his wife and daughter stood on the bookshelf. Would his Ann still be smiling at him today if she saw what he had become? He knew she wouldn't.

"Okay, Ann, I'll stop trying to come to you," he said out loud to the picture.

Maybe I have been doing this backward all this time, he muttered to himself.

Looking around the living room, he wondered if he would have time to clean up before she arrived. It could be today. It could be weeks from now. Why didn't she tell him when?

Not for the first time, he could have sworn he heard his wife's voice.

"It's about time, Tommy," she said.

But this time, he stopped pretending that he didn't hear her. This time he answered, "Yes, it is."

This time he didn't care if it was really his wife or if he was crazy or making it up because he missed her so much. It didn't matter anymore. What mattered is that he get ready.

Fours hours later, the dishes were washed. The living room was picked up, and the guest bedroom that he hadn't gone into for years was vacuumed and dusted. It was a beginning.

And Thomas realized that he was hungry. Really hungry. He and Maggie used to go to the Diner in town. He wondered if it was still there. But he couldn't go the way he was. It was time to clean himself up. Looking at the pile of dirty clothes by the washer, he scooped them up into a trash bag.

Rags, he told himself.

Although Thomas thought he would never wear work clothes again, he had kept them. Not because he thought he would need them, but because he was too lazy to throw them out.

They'll work, for now, he told himself.

An hour later, showered, shaved, and dressed in clothes that almost fit him, Thomas didn't recognize himself when he looked in the mirror. Brushing his white hair back into a ponytail, he decided the first thing to do was get a haircut. Then food.

It was mid-afternoon by the time Thomas walked into the Diner. He had been hungry for hours, but he had decided he wanted to be presentable to the world before he joined it again. The little bell above the door tinkled as he walked in, and he smiled, remembering how much Maggie liked that sound.

The Diner looked almost the same as he remembered. But the man who welcomed him was someone he had never met before. Tall, broad-shouldered, kind brown eyes and a welcoming smile. It was hard not to smile back at him.

"Welcome," Pete said.

Behind the counter, Pete's wife, Barbara, smiled. Whoever this was that just walked into the Diner was bringing a story with him. It didn't take any magical gifts to know that. She couldn't wait to hear it.

SIX

M aya didn't really have a job—at least not the type of job that
Ginny assumed her mother was going to each morning.
Maya had evaded Ginny's desire to visit her at work or learn what
she did for so long that Ginny no longer asked.

Maya didn't need to work for money. Akotas had made sure she
would always have enough, and neither Dradon nor Isira took that
away from her. Dradon, because he knew she needed money to live,
and Isira because they had once been friends. Maya snorted at the
thought of the three siblings that became her family. Some family.

At least I have Ginny, Maya mused, as she maneuvered her rusted
heap of a car through the traffic to where she would spend her day.

Maya drove away every morning to a job she didn't have, or need,
to fool Ginny, so Ginny wouldn't worry. And, Maya admitted to
herself, to give herself something to do other than sit alone in the
house, too afraid to do anything other than hope Ginny would
make a happy life for herself.

The trouble was, Ginny was not doing that. And now Maya
worried her daughter would never make a life for herself because
she believed she needed to take care of her sick mother.

Maya sighed. This life was not the life she once dreamed about.
She once expected she would live a magic life. Well, it had magic,

just not the magic Maya once wanted. But then, how could she have known?

She had been an ordinary girl living with normal parents who worked regular jobs until that day when Akotas arrived out of nowhere.

That day, Maya was angry as always at her parents and the boredom of her life. She had gone to her favorite place to ponder how to change her life. Something that would differ from the life that loomed in front of her. She wanted adventure, and that day she was desperate.

The fighting at home was terrible. Her studies at school bored her, and she was considering either dropping out or changing her major at the University to something like Greek Myths and Legends. Perhaps by learning about them, she would look at the world differently and then live a vicariously adventurous life.

However, Maya understood that either choice would upset her parents. She lived at home because they had barely scraped the money together to send her to college. She knew what they would say if she changed her major to something so impractical.

"How can you make money with that kind of education? We haven't worked our entire lives for you to do something that frivolous!"

"Well, why do they have these classes then?" she'd ask her parents. "They must be there for a reason."

"They are for rich people," her father would answer. "People like us don't study just for fun."

The last time she discussed this with her parents, she had hugged them both and thanked them for their advice, even though Maya realized she would not follow it. But she loved them for what they had done for her, and she hated that if she lived life her way, she would hurt their feelings and disappoint them.

Leo Gibbons ran his hands through his hair, smoothing it back. He liked what he saw in the mirror. Everyone did. Well, almost everyone.

Some people could see his black heart. But most people just liked the way he looked. Not tall, dark, and handsome. Tall, blond, and beautiful. Those are the words he said to himself every morning. He'd been doing it as long as he could remember, even when he was short. Just a kid. He would look in the mirror and see himself grown up. Ready to take on the world, and his looks would be one of his tools.

Winking at himself, with one of his deep green eyes, he smiled. It was a perfect smile. It hadn't always been. Fighting as a child had chipped his front tooth, and bad water had yellowed them. As soon as he had money, he had them all capped. Now they shone white and straight. He had trained himself to smile, so that there were tiny smile lines by his lips, and he allowed his eyes to squint just the perfect amount so his smile would appear genuine.

It was. Always. But never for the reason people thought it was. He was always in control.

Right, he said to himself, *always.*

Except for now. For a moment, two parallel lines formed between his eyes as he frowned. Seeing the lines in the mirror, he stopped frowning with his face, but that didn't stop his anger.

As he stood in front of the mirror, he practiced allowing the anger to simmer, almost to the boiling point, while his face gave nothing away. The hardest part was his eyes. They had to emit warmth. He had no warmth. Especially not for Alice. He only had hatred. When he found her, he would enjoy letting her experience what a black heart could do. After all, she already knew he had one. That's why she had run away.

If she had just run away, it wouldn't have been that bad. But she did more than leave him. She took something valuable.

A sneer passed over Leo's features as he took one last look in the mirror. He wiped it away completely. He'd save it for later when he checked in with Ace. He had assigned Ace to get to know his daughter. Really get to know her. Find out where she had hidden what she took.

He had thought that was a kinder way to deal with his daughter than he usually dealt with people that disappointed him.

Like her mother. God, she had been a beauty. Wild, crazy—a passionate beauty. Yes, an incredible woman with a nasty habit. Snooping.

Leo sighed. He missed her. Yes, he had any woman he wanted. Men too, but in a different way. But she was the one. She was his soul mate. But the day he found her packing her bags, with little Alice standing beside her with tears in her eyes, he knew he couldn't keep her anymore.

"Where are you going?" he asked, picking up Alice. His wife, Maggie, turned with red-rimmed eyes and said, "I thought I would take Alice home to meet my dad."

Yes, Maggie could look into his eyes and see his black heart. She had loved him anyway. But that day, he knew she was lying. There was something else going on.

When he asked, she said, "No. I just miss him. It's been years. He doesn't even know about Alice. We won't be gone long," he knew she was lying.

He wanted to scream. Instead, he said, "I wish you would have let me know. I would have gone with you."

It was the slight pause before she said, "I'm sorry. Would you like to come with us?" that told him she was running away. She had thought he would not be back until the morning, and she and Alice would be long gone.

He had no idea who Maggie's father was. They had never talked about family. He didn't want to know about hers, and she didn't want to know about his. She knew he had other women. She knew he ran a business that brought them lots of money, but she hadn't cared.

What had changed, he asked himself that day. Because this was no longer the woman who didn't care, this was a woman who had only one thing on her mind. Get away from him as fast as possible.

"Oh, honey, I would love to come," he had said, holding Alice even tighter.

He could still feel her arms around his neck, saying, "Daddy, come with us."

"I can't. I'm sorry. How are you getting there?"

"Flying," Maggie had whispered, knowing he would understand that she was desperate to leave.

"Perfect," he had answered. "I have a few free hours. Let me drive you to the airport."

"I called a taxi," she said.

"No problem. I'll pay him when he gets here and take you myself. That way, we have a few more minutes together."

"Goody," Alice had said. "Thanks, Daddy."

A few hours later, he and Alice stood in the hospital together and cried. Alice was hugging his neck once again. But this time, she was sobbing, making his shirt wet. Leo had patted her back, letting tears gather in his eyes as he answered questions about what had happened.

Yes, a deer had run out onto the road. He had swerved to miss it and gone into the lake. He had managed to free himself and get his daughter out.

He thought his wife was right behind him. But—his voice caught as he continued—Maggie didn't come out of the lake. The car was gone. He stumbled to the road and flagged down a car. By the time the emergency crews arrived, it was too late.

"Yes," he told the police, "I am available anytime. But please, may I take my daughter home?"

"Is there anyone we can call for you?" they had asked.

"No," he had replied with tears in his eyes and a sob in his voice. "There isn't. It's just Alice and me."

Sixteen years later. It was just him. But first, he had to find the daughter who had turned out to be too much like her mother even if she didn't look like her.

SEVEN

E vie slept in. She was in a safe place. And she was exhausted. Every few hours, she would wake up, look at the red lights of the digital clock, say to herself, just a few more hours, and snuggle down even deeper into her bag. She had until eleven to check out, and she was going to use every minute of them.

Without admitting it to herself, she hoped that she would remember again when she woke up. Or at least dream about it and remember it then. But she didn't dream, and she didn't remember. Her memory was still missing.

Finally, hunger drove her to sit up. She reached over and grabbed a cold piece of pizza, lifted the lid of the ice bucket that now held only cold water, and took out a dripping can of soda. She popped the lid, took a bite of pizza, a long swig of soda and sighed.

If she could keep herself from trying to remember if she used to do this before and accepted this is what Evie Lynne did now, it felt great. She might like this new person she was becoming. Evie clicked on the TV and found the screen that told her the date. Last night she had been afraid to ask anyone, and nothing in the motel lobby or the pizza shop gave it away.

It was October. Did she like this time of year? She decided that she did. She didn't bother listening to the news. What good would it do her? But it was time to get moving.

The first thing she needed was a map. A trail map would be best, or at least something that showed her how to walk to Pennsylvania without being near a major highway or city. If she had enough money, she'd keep walking. If she ran out, she'd get work.

She had slept without clothes because she had washed everything. Almost everything was dry, and a few minutes with the blow dryer did the trick.

She took one more shower—who knew when she would get another chance—dressed, and repacked her bag. One last glance in the mirror reminded her that her roots were showing. Eventually, she would need to dye her hair again. She could see why she had done it in the first place. Red hair was something people remembered.

The pizza boy said the town was down the road. She'd get more food, a map, some hair dye, and be on her way.

· · · · ● · ● · · ·

Owen Riley, the pizza boy, watched the woman from last night walk by. He had stayed the night in the back of the shop. He had no other place to sleep. Working part-time at a pizza place didn't give him enough money to pay rent anywhere, and the owner of the shop didn't mind. He figured that it helped keep the place safe, and as long as no one else knew about it, and if he couldn't tell that Owen had slept there when he came into work every afternoon, then he didn't care.

Owen had been in the process of opening the shop for the day when he saw her. She looked so free. He turned and looked back into the shop and already knew what his next twenty-four hours would look like. Heck, he knew what his next twenty-four years would look like.

Someday the owner would tell him he could buy him out, and he would run this dinky shop in the middle of nowhere until one day he would wake up and he would look just like the owner: old, pizza heavy, with a wife and kids he never saw anymore.

A wave of despair flooded Owen. The smell of old pizza, sticky soda, and something from the bathroom, was all he could smell, and he panicked.

Turning back to see the woman, now almost out of sight, he did something he never would have thought he could do. He decided this would not be his life.

Flinging himself out the door, he yelled, "Wait!'

When she didn't turn, he ran, yelling, "Wait, please wait. Just one minute."

Evie turned, startled to see the pizza boy running towards her. What could he possibly want? She was tired of pizza. But she waited.

By the time he reached her, he was panting. Bending over, hands on his knees, he tried to talk. But all that came out was a stammer of "please."

Evie stared at the boy, waiting as patiently as she could. She was a little afraid that they were standing by a road where everyone could see them, fearful that perhaps he had figured out who she was and had been sent to collect her.

But when he straightened up, she could see tears running down his cheeks, and she knew it was something else.

"Please," he said, angrily brushing the tears away, upset he was this weak. "Please, let me go with you."

"What? No!" Evie said, and turned away.

"Please. I need to be someone else. Let me go with you. Please."

The last "please" had Owen leaning over again panic catching his breath.

"I promise not to be a problem. You'll be safer with me, anyway. Please."

Evie turned and looked again at the boy.

"How old are you?"

"Eighteen."

"Prove it."

Reaching into his back pocket, Owen produced a driver's license. Evie squinted in the sunlight at what it said. Owen Riley. Eighteen as of April 13th.

"Why?"

"I have nothing. I sleep at the pizza shop. I will never get to leave here. If you don't like me being with you, you can leave me somewhere. But at least let me walk with you for a while."

Evie's mind raced. No one would be looking for a woman and her brother. They looked enough alike that they could be family. Besides, he knew where they were. And he could drive.

"Okay. We'll try it out. But I will leave you if it doesn't work out."

"Five minutes. Could you wait for me for five minutes?"

When Evie nodded, he turned and ran back to the pizza shop.

Evie watched him go, thinking this was a crazy idea. But her heart went out to him. She was missing who she was, and he would miss out on life if she didn't take him with her. And she could leave him if she had to.

She wondered if she had a real brother somewhere who would be glad this boy was with her. If not, now she had one. All part of making a new life for herself.

EIGHT

Thomas pointed to his favorite table by the window and was given the nod of okay by the man who had greeted him. Sliding into the seat that felt so familiar, Thomas smiled.

He looked out onto the town's park and realized he had missed its renovation. A pergola now stood in one corner, and there were more benches than he remembered being there before.

Pete saw him looking out the window and said, "They did such a good job of fixing that park up, didn't they?

"Hi, I'm Pete Mann." Pointing to Barbara, he added, "That's my wife, Barbara."

"Are you the owners?" Thomas asked.

"We are. We bought this place a few years ago. Best decision of my life! Do you know what you want to eat?" Pete asked.

"Not new in town. Used to come here all the time. They used to make good hamburgers."

"We still make good hamburgers. Let me make you one. And some fries?"

Thomas nodded yes and then realized that he hadn't introduced himself.

"Sorry, I'm Thomas Hendrick."

"Nice to meet you, Thomas," Pete replied. "Let me get your food started."

While Pete cooked, Barbara came over and asked Thomas what he would like to drink. She brought his coke over in a can with a glass with ice, just the way he used to get his drinks when he and his daughter Maggie would come for lunch.

A wave of sadness came over him, and he gasped at how much it hurt to remember. No wonder he had worked so hard to forget.

Barbara put her hand on his shoulder and asked, "Are you okay?"

Dabbing at his eyes with his napkin, he answered, "I'm not sure."

Barbara pulled out a chair and sat across from him. "Do you need someone to talk to? I have time to listen."

Thomas looked at the woman across from him with her kind eyes and at her husband cooking his hamburger and said, "I think I do."

Barbara stood and pulled down the Diner's blinds. Glancing at her husband who nodded at her, she turned the signs from open to closed and then locked the front door.

"But your customers?" Thomas asked.

"Mid-afternoon break," Barbara said, "We do it all the time."

Thomas gave her a wan smile as Pete brought his food to the table. Suddenly he was not only extraordinarily hungry but anxious to tell his story as well.

Once again, Barbara anticipated his needs and said, "Pete and I will clean up the kitchen. You eat. When you're done, we can talk."

It was all he could do not to cry. Him. He never cried. He couldn't afford it. But since his wife had died, he had trusted no one to help him, and here he was talking to two strangers and getting ready to tell them everything. Barbara drifted off, acting as if nothing had happened, and he turned to the task of eating. He knew that eating would probably also help his emotional state.

That turned out to be true. By the time Barbara came to collect his plates and bring another soda and a slice of cherry pie for each of them, he felt like a new man.

While they ate pie, Thomas asked Pete and Barbara questions about when they had bought the Diner. Pete took time to explain how he had been a long-distance trucker hired to take a hitchhiker to California.

The hitchhiker was a woman named Ava Anders. She lived in Doveland and needed to get to Los Angeles. After all the ensuing adventures, they became friends, and Ava and her husband and friends had invited him and Barbara to move to Doveland. Then they helped them buy the Diner.

"It's been a dream come true," Barbara said, reaching out to hold Pete's hand. "We have found the most amazing friends, Doveland is beautiful, and we have had time to be together after all the years of Pete working and me being home with the kids."

Pete smiled at his wife.

"True! And we have had many more adventures since moving here, helping people mostly. That is the part we love the most. Perhaps we can be of help to you? That is, if you are willing to share your story."

Thomas sighed and poured soda into his glass, watching it run down over the ice cubes, causing tiny cracks. He felt like the ice cube—and Pete and Barbara were causing tiny cracks in him. No, it was the letter that started it.

He reached into his jacket, pulled out the letter, and handed it to Pete, saying, "This came to me today."

Pete carefully unfolded the letter that Thomas had folded up into a square and, with Barbara reading it over his shoulder, read what it said. It didn't take long. There wasn't much to it after all.

Pete handed the letter back. "She didn't say much, did she? But still, you must be excited to see her. How long has it been?"

"That's the thing," Thomas said. "I've never met her. I didn't even know I had a granddaughter."

Barbara stopped herself from saying, "Oh, you must be so excited," because that didn't seem the direction that Thomas was going with this.

"How do you feel about it?" she asked, instead.

Thomas glanced away and turned back, having decided to tell the whole truth.

"I don't know. I guess that's what I need help with."

"Well, you have come to the right place, Thomas. We are all ears, and we will help any way we can."

For a moment, Thomas swore he heard his wife say, "I'm proud of you, Tommy."

But he dismissed it. No need to tell these friendly people that. They would probably think he was crazy and run the other way, and now that he had decided he wanted and needed friends, he didn't want to lose them.

NINE

Ace had been very clear with Leo. Yes, he would find Alice. No, she had not told him anything. Not about leaving. Not about anything. Including her family.

Of course, he tried to get information from her. But she only said that her father and mother had died.

Yes, he knew that Leo was her father, but he couldn't tell her he knew that, could he?

Sure he had an idea where she had gone.

Of course, both he and Leo knew that he was lying. He had no idea where Alice had gone. But then he and Leo were adept at lying. It turned out, so was Alice.

Ace had tried every way that he could think of to get her to tell him about her childhood. Her parents. Of course, he knew the answer to all those questions, so he also knew that she was lying. But what could he say?

"Hey, I know your father, Leo Gibbons. Hey, I know that your mother died trying to run away from him. Now you have run away too, and your evil father thinks you know something or have something that will ruin everything for him."

Was that what he was going to say to her to get her to talk? But somewhere along the way, he must have given himself away because she was truly and completely gone.

Not like the last time when she kicked him out because he slapped her. First, she had hit him back and kicked him in the family jewels, and in his weakened state, pushed him out the front door and locked it.

He hadn't moved in yet, so only his toothbrush was at her house, and he didn't have a key, so it was no big deal.

He was sick of her, anyway. But when he called Leo to tell him that it hadn't worked. That his daughter knew nothing, had nothing, and he had done his job, Leo had stopped talking.

Ace could feel daggers of hate coming through the phone, along with a freezing silence. Ace was so terrified he froze, afraid of saying anything.

How could someone send that much fear through a phone line, Ace thought later. Perhaps he had imagined it. But he knew that he hadn't.

After what seemed an eternity, Leo spoke only three words: "Get her back." The meaning was crystal clear.

It was not in his nature to grovel, which is how he saw it, but he did it. He sent flowers. He begged. He promised to go to anger management classes. Please give him another chance. Didn't the names Ace and Alice go together well? Didn't that mean something?

It had taken months, but finally Alice agreed to see him again. Slowly, slowly, he had won his way back into her heart. He had been the perfect boyfriend. Still, he learned nothing. And Leo started threatening that he would take care of it on his own.

That thought terrified even him. Yes, Alice was Leo's daughter, which was probably why he had done nothing to her in the first place. Ace knew Leo's reputation. He had no boundaries. No rules.

And even though he hadn't meant to, he had developed feelings, maybe small ones, but actual feelings for Alice. She murmured in her sleep. He recorded it, hoping it told him something. All it told him was something terrible had happened to her mother. He already knew that. Now, if he didn't find Alice soon, something terrible would happen to him, too.

Now that Alice was gone, Ace started to think that she had been buying time. Maybe she knew who Ace was, that he worked for her father.

If that were true, what had Alice done during those months? Perhaps if he started there, he could figure out where she was going. Maybe get there before she did.

The best place to ask questions was at her work. She must have told them something. He'd start there.

• • • • • • • • • •

"Are you going anywhere in particular?" Owen asked. "I mean, are we going anywhere in particular?"

Evie looked at the young boy in front of her. Too thin, slightly stooped, maybe from making pizza, perhaps from worry, and wondered what she had got herself into. Was she a caretaker? Was she capable of helping this person?

"Is there someone who needs to know that you are leaving? Family, friends, your work?"

Owen shook his head. "I left a note at the pizza shop. He will only care that he has to find someone else to do all the work. I shouldn't say anything mean like that. He did let me sleep there."

The two of them were walking towards town using a path alongside the highway that Owen said he used all the time. Evie didn't want anyone to see her, and Owen seemed to feel the same way.

"Will he come after you?" She asked.

"He might drive down the road looking for me. Maybe out of worry, but probably to get me to come back and make lunch."

"And there is no one else?"

"People from high school who know my name. That's it."

"You know I am asking you about your parents. Where are they? Won't they care?"

"No. I sleep at the pizza shop because they locked me out of the house. Told me I am an abomination and until I repented, I was not theirs."

Evie stopped and looked at Owen. "An abomination?"

"Look," Owen said, "I'm gay. Now, are you going to abandon me too? Tell me to walk alone. Really? Just join the crowd. Go ahead. Say it."

Evie stared at Owen, seeing the fire in his eyes, his back straighten, and thought, "Ah, there he is!"

"No."

"No, what?"

"Not doing any of that. What difference does it make that you're gay? Maybe I am, who knows? Let's get to town and get supplies and get away from the road."

Evie turned and walked away. Owen stared at her back, wondering what she meant when she said, "who knows." What did she mean by that?

"Let's go," Evie called back to him.

Owen didn't wait for her to call again. Whatever was going on with this woman, he would help. He liked that she made nothing of what he said. He didn't want to be fawned over. He wanted a purpose. And he had a feeling that this woman was leading him toward it.

TEN

By the time the pie was finished, so was Thomas' story. His wife died in childbirth. He raised his daughter Maggie on his own, but obviously, he had done a piss-poor job of it.

She had started running with the wrong crowd. Started smoking. Acting out. Then someone got her hooked on drugs, and that was the beginning of the end.

She left the day she turned eighteen. He figured she went with one of the boys in town, but doubted that she stayed with him. She was ambitious. Not in the way he had been ambitious. He wanted to succeed at his job, which he did. Maybe one reason he hadn't succeeded as a father.

No, her ambition was to be someone. But not by working at it. By finding it and latching on to it. His heart broke again when she left. First, his wife, then his daughter. It devastated him.

He spent money trying to find her. But there were no clues, no hints of where she had gone. He figured somewhere out west. He doubted she would have stayed in the cold. She hated the cold. So maybe California?

Here Thomas paused and looked out the window. He looked back at his coke, at the ice cubes melting, and sighed. Pete and Barbara waited with compassion in their eyes.

41

"You said you have kids?"

"Two," Barbara answered. "They grew up and have lives of their own."

Thomas nodded.

"I guess that makes it a little easier. You saw them build a life of their own. Instead, Maggie just left. Over twenty years ago. I have been alone ever since. Once my job was over, so was my life. I had poured all of myself into my work, and then there was nothing left. I've just been waiting to die, hoping it would be soon. Until this morning when I got the letter.

"Something turned on inside of me. Something I thought I had lost. I have a purpose. I want to be ready to help her—this Alice—when she arrives. I cleaned myself up and came for food, and now here I am."

Thomas spread his arms wide, taking in the Diner and Pete and Barbara.

"And I have no idea what to do next. How is she coming? When? What does she want? How did she find me? Did Maggie tell her? Is Maggie still alive? These are questions I have no answer to. All I know is I can't ruin my relationship with her the way I did with her mother."

While Thomas talked, Pete and Barbara listened. They nodded and smiled and encouraged him to go on, being careful not to interject anything that would distract or worry him.

"You won't, Thomas," Barbara said, taking both his hands in hers. "She's coming because she wants to see you. And whenever she gets here, you will be ready. Even if it's today."

"Today?" Thomas said, standing up. "I'm not ready."

"You are ready," Pete said. "But since it's unlikely that your Alice is coming today, let's make good use of the time to get even more ready. What would you like to prepare for her?"

Thomas sat down, paused, and then looked up.

"The house. I haven't taken care of it at all since Maggie left, and I had already neglected it after my wife died."

At that moment, there was a quiet knock on the glass door of the Diner.

Pete turned to look at who knocked and then laughed. Barbara joined in.

"Ask, and you shall receive," Barbara said to a puzzled Thomas.

Pete had already opened the door and led the man over to the table.

"Hank, meet Thomas Hendrick. Thomas was just mentioning that he needs some work done on his house. Thomas, this is Hank Blaze. Carpenter, and all-around good guy."

At those words, Hank blushed. He tried to hide it, but Barbara, seeing it, patted him on his back. She knew that Hank had only begun to believe that he was a good guy.

He had lived a life of crime for many years before finding Ava, the hitchhiker who her husband had helped. Ava, Hank's niece. One he didn't know he had. And once he did, his life had changed.

There were definite similarities in their stories. Hank had found a niece he didn't know he had, and it had changed his entire life. Thomas had learned of a granddaughter he didn't know he had, and it had already started to change his life, too.

"Sit down, Hank, and we'll tell you what's going on?" She replied.

After hearing what Thomas had in mind for his house, Hank said, "I'm your man. We just finished a project, and I have a crew ready and willing to get started on something else."

Thomas looked at Pete and Barbara and shook his head.

"Are you all like this?"

Hank laughed. "I'm the worse of them. Just wait until you meet the others. If you are ready, why not take me over to your house now and show me what you want to have done so I can get the materials we need to get started."

Thomas rose and started to follow Hank out the door and then turned and returned to Pete and Barbara.

"Thank you so much. You have no idea what this means to me. And I feel a little embarrassed to be asking this, but when can I meet the others that Hank referred to?"

Hank had stopped at the door to wait for Thomas, and hearing Thomas' question, Hank raised his finger to signal for them to wait and then made a phone call.

"Tonight at Ava's," he said. "She said to come at 6:00 p.m. She already was making a ton of food. Bring Grace too, she said. I'll bring Thomas."

After the two of them went out the door, Barbara opened the blinds and turned the sign back to open. Pete made a few phone calls. First to his cook Alex Bender to ask if he could come into work, and then to two servers who always were looking for extra work. Yes, they would all be delighted and would be there within the hour.

Barbara called Grace. Pete could hear the squeal of happiness across the room. Grace loved a good story and a chance to help. Another adventure had begun.

Pete put his arm around his wife, and they watched out the window as Thomas pointed out his car so that Hank could follow him.

"Do you think his granddaughter is bringing good news?" Barbara asked.

"I think she is coming to get help," Pete answered.

"And we'll be ready," she answered.

ELEVEN

A few minutes down the road, Evie turned to look at what Owen had brought with him and shook her head.

"That's it?"

Owen stood in front of her, legs spread, arms crossed over his body, his blue eyes locked into hers, and answered as confidently as he could.

"Yes."

Evie laughed, and then seeing Owen's stance wilt, she put her hand on his arm and said, "Sorry, Owen. But picking you up is like finding a mongrel dog by the side of the road and realizing that they are now your responsibility. Not something I was expecting."

Owen shifted the bag he was carrying on his back and turned to walk away. Evie caught his hand and stopped him. She walked around until she was face to face with him.

"I laughed, not out of upset, or at you, but because at that moment, I realized I needed a friend. And I think rescuing mongrel dogs from the side of the road might have been something I liked to do."

The two of them stood facing each other, almost eye to eye, for a few more seconds until something shifted in Owen, and he said, "You think you might have enjoyed doing that?"

"A long story, my friend," Evie said, "Or maybe a short one. But not one that I can tell you now. We need to get you some supplies. Is there some kind of camping supply store in town?"

"Yes, but that means we are going to camp?"

"Mostly. In a few days, I might have you rent a car. But not here where people know you."

"So you are hiding?"

"That I am."

"From what?"

"Another story, Owen. No time right now. Let's get supplies and get out of town before nightfall. I also need a trail map. Is there a place where we can get onto the Internet?"

"Nothing in town. But I could go back to the pizza shop and use the computer. If I hurry back, we have time. Unless the owner checks in at lunch, which he rarely does."

Evie took Owen's pack. Pointing at a patch of woods by the road, she said, "I'll wait for you there. If he comes back, keep working. Leave when he does. Don't act suspicious. But print out trail maps that would take us from here to Doveland, Pennsylvania. It's near Pittsburgh."

"Okay, you promise you'll wait for me?"

"Yes! Now go."

Owen ran back to the shop as Evie made her way to the woods. He turned and ran back. "Did you say Pennsylvania?"

"Yes! Get going!"

"We are walking to Pennsylvania? Are you kidding?"

"Why, where are we?"

"Oregon, near Idaho. How could you not know?"

Evie just pointed towards the shop, and Owen shook his head and started running.

Evie shook her head too. How did she not know? That was the question.

• • • ● • ● • ● • • •

Ace's search for Alice at work turned out to be fruitless. More than fruitless. Fiction.

All this time, Ace thought, *all this time she has been playing me.*

The fury he had felt before was a small ember compared to how he felt now. He thought he had actually felt something for her, which had both surprised him and scared him.

He had never really liked a woman before as much as he had liked Alice. It frightened him because he might feel compelled to defend her against whatever Leo had in mind. And Leo was one scary dude.

There was a tiny part of Ace that had thought if he could assure Leo that Alice knew nothing, then perhaps he would let her alone. And since he had believed that Alice cared for him, he had thought that maybe he could reform himself so they could live a normal life together. Maybe have kids. Or not.

But now. Now Ace realized that Leo knew his daughter better than he had. She was a conniving, scheming little bitch. Now he wanted to find her for himself, too.

But he couldn't tell Leo anything about what Alice had done. Because knowing Leo, he would probably think that Ace was in on it. Actually, he wouldn't think it, Leo would assume it, and since Ace was not the only one that worked for Leo, someone else would take care of both of them. And Ace was easy to find.

That meant he had to hide too while he searched for Alice. The movie "Alice doesn't live here anymore" popped into his mind.

Not only didn't Alice live here anymore, but it also turned out that she never did.

It was more like the reason Alice's mother had named her Alice in the first place. She had named her after Alice in Wonderland.

Alice's mother, Maggie, had wanted Alice to know there was more to life than what her father had told her.

It turned out that it was precisely what Alice had learned. She had fallen down the rabbit hole, and now he had to follow her down. Where did it start?

They lived in Oregon because Alice loved to hike, and Oregon and Idaho had lots of places to do that. Did she take a trail, and which one was it?

Alice would have picked one that he would find challenging to make it harder for him to find her. However, he didn't have to hike. He just had to turn up where each trail came to a town because he knew she would walk light and buy supplies as she went along.

Ace sat at his computer and pulled up trail guides.

Just pick one, he told himself. *Pretend, you are Alice, hiding from everyone. Heading away. Where would I go?*

The vague memory of Alice telling him that her mother came from Pennsylvania surfaced. It was the best chance he had. He picked a town on the road heading east, hoping for the best.

TWELVE

As always, when the word got around that there was a gathering at Ava's, everyone who could be there showed up. So Ava wasn't surprised that Johnny and Lex came with their mother, Valerie. Valerie's new husband, Craig Lester, came in his own car. Craig was the town's doctor, and he never knew when there would be an emergency and he'd have to rush off.

And, as always, no one came empty-handed. So although Ava had made enough food to feed a small army, as her husband Evan said teasing her about the state of the kitchen, even more food arrived as each car pulled up.

Hank and Thomas were the last to arrive. Hank had made detailed lists of things he needed to do to bring Thomas' house back to life. Hank made calls to his crew, arranging for what needed immediate attention.

After listing all the necessary repairs, Hank asked Thomas if there was anything he ever wanted in the house he didn't have. After a moment of hesitation, head bowed to the ground, Thomas said that there was. His wife had dreamed of a covered back deck and a garden. Could that happen?

"Absolutely," Hank had said, making notes of who he had in mind that could help.

Thankfully, two key players would be at Ava's.

At 6:00 p.m., Evan texted Hank to get himself and the guest of honor to the house. Hank laughed. He used to have an evil boss who told him what to do. Now he had friends who reminded him of what to do.

Hank drove Thomas to the house, promising to take him home after dinner. They both had a long day ahead of them in the morning. Before they left, Thomas wrote a note and pinned it to the door.

"What if Alice comes while I'm away? I put my phone number on it so she can call me."

Thomas held up the small phone Hank had helped him buy. It was a disposable phone, but it would do for the moment until he got him to a store to get him a permanent one.

"Now, I have to learn how to use it."

The phone had been Thomas' idea. He had never bothered to get a mobile phone. There was no one to call, and he never left home.

Now, as part of his return to the land of the living, he would not always be home. He had been only joking about not knowing how to use it. Technology had been his thing until he stopped working and stayed home to die.

Yes, he was a few years behind, but it would not take long to catch up, he promised himself. Once Alice came home, he would never want to be out of touch with her.

Before stepping out of the car, Thomas turned to Hank and said, "I'm nervous."

"Well, who the heck wouldn't be," Hank said. "But not to worry, Grace will be there to smooth over the rough bumps."

At Thomas' look, Hank added.

"Grace Strong. Her name says it all. Grace owns the coffee shop across from the Diner. You'll have to visit it. Sit there long enough, and everyone in town will show up. She didn't name it Your Second Home for nothing. That's what it feels like.

"So Grace is the woman that knows everyone. Except you. That shows how hidden away you have been. So let's take care of that right now."

"Take care of what right now," Grace said, arriving at the moment they both stepped out of the car.

"Meeting you, of course," Hank said. After he introduced them, he excused himself and walked around the house to the bunkhouse. Although Hank had his own home in Concourse, he always kept a room in Ava and Evan's bunkhouse for times like this. He wanted to change clothes and freshen up before dinner.

Grace hooked her arm around Thomas and said, "It's my job to introduce you to everyone."

Thomas looked down at the woman standing beside him. Short dark gray hair and deep brown eyes. Glasses on a chain, fashionable but comfortable clothes, and a smile that felt like sunshine on a dreary day. Tears came to his eyes, and he looked away.

Grace stopped and smiled at him. "I understand, you know. My husband, Eric, the love of my life, passed away recently."

Thomas didn't have time to ask how she knew how he felt before she brought him into the house. A large open room lay before him. People sat on couches and chairs, and since he could see into the kitchen, he could also see others gathered around a tall woman with her hair in a ponytail directing the preparation of the food.

"Yes, that's Ava, Hank's niece. Shall we walk around the room?"

Thomas realized that he didn't actually have a choice. Grace was a force of nature, determined to have him know everyone and be comfortable at the same time.

By the time they had walked the room, the table was ready, and everyone had found their seat. He was, not surprisingly and gratefully, seated next to Grace.

He used to run meetings where he had to remember everyone's name, so while they paused in silence to say whatever form of grace they each wanted, Thomas tested himself to see if he remembered their names.

Grace, of course. Hank had arrived and sat on the other side of him. Then Pete and Barbara across the table. Ava and her husband, Evan, on opposite sides of the circle, making sure everyone was taken care of. Ben, their son, sat in a booster chair beside Ava and was busy smashing peas with his open palm and licking it off. Thomas tried not to laugh at the sight.

What if they all ate their peas that way?

Then Craig, the doctor, and his wife Valerie, who used to be a teacher and the high school principal. Now, she ran a design firm out of their house.

Grace had told him Valerie was also the head of the Town Council and responsible for many of the improvements in town, including the upgraded town park that he had noticed.

Their younger son, Lex, sat beside them. Their other son, Johnny, sat directly across from him. And it was Johnny that unnerved him. It was something about the way he was looking at him. But then Johnny winked, and Thomas nodded back at him.

After dinner, they would want to know his story, but the way they acted, he wondered how many of them already knew it. How, he didn't know. But Johnny's wink had given it away.

THIRTEEN

Almost two thousand miles away, the object of the story was trying to calm herself.

Evie had seen a car pull in with the name "The Pizza Shop" on its side and realized that the owner had showed up after all. That meant that Owen was stuck, at least until the owner left.

So she moved further back into the woods and, putting both packs beside her, leaned back onto the trunk of a massive oak tree. She realized that it was probably good that she had this time to think through what was happening. Instead of walking into town without thinking, they needed to prepare.

It wasn't a big town, but it still could have cameras. And people could recognize Owen. And since she didn't know who she was hiding from, it would be best to assume they knew what they were doing and might be intelligent enough to put a missing teenager and a missing woman together.

And now that she knew where they were, she realized she was out of her mind thinking they could walk across the country.

What had she been thinking? Did she think that was the safest way, or had she another plan? Was she going to rent a car? If so, with what?

She had no identification at all on her. Just a wad of cash. Had she stashed information elsewhere? Or was she in too big of a hurry? Or was she just stupid?

Evie banged her head softly against the tree.

If only I could remember, she thought. *It would make all of this so much easier.*

Why had she forgotten who she was but remembered everything else? She realized that now she remembered the name of this tree. How come? What did she do in her actual life? The life that she had before she started walking or running away?

No matter, she said to herself. *I have to assume I'm not stupid, and stupid would be walking. Now that I have help, we can rent a car. It will still take us time to get across the country. But not months of walking. I couldn't have been thinking that. I must have planned to only walk to where no one would know me. So now we only have to walk to where no one would know Owen and rent a car.*

This line of reasoning made sense to Evie.

She'd ask Owen how they could get to another town, and that would be their plan. She hoped it wasn't too far. They had to get there before nightfall since Owen couldn't stay out in the woods without equipment.

Evie closed her eyes to wait for Owen, feeling more relieved than she had since she had woken up without a memory. Was that only yesterday? It felt like years.

A few minutes later, she heard Owen softly call her name. She whispered, "here," and then stood so Owen could see her. A wave of fear ran through her when she saw that Owen wasn't alone.

"No," she said and turned to look where she could run.

"No," the man said, putting his hand out to stop her. "I'm here to help."

Owen nodded. "He saw my note before I could hide it. We talked. He wants to help me. Which means help you, too."

Evie looked back and forth between the two of them. In a million years, she would have never asked this man for help, but he stood there with tears in his eyes, hand outstretched. Owen was standing beside him, grinning from ear to ear.

"Why?"

"I told the entire story to Owen, but the short version is that years ago my wife took my son and daughter from me. I deserved it. I've never been able to find them. But I pray that they are well and that the kindness of strangers has helped them along the way.

"I can't hope that for them if I don't do the same for you and Owen. I know he has no future here. He's the best employee I've ever had. And the kind of man I hope my son has become."

Evie looked away. It seemed real. Why not let him help?

The man broke into her thoughts.

"I know you are running from someone. Let me rent you a car to get you where you want to go. No one will look for it in my name. I'll close the shop for a week and say I am going on a trip. That way, no one will wonder why I rented a car. All I ask is that you let me know that you are both safe when you get wherever you are going."

When Evie still didn't respond, he said, "Please. Let me do this for you. Please."

Owen didn't say please out loud, but his face gave him away.

When she said, "Okay," both of them started beaming.

"Here's the plan," the man said. "Owen will drop me off at the car rental place and then come back here. I'll bring the car to you. Or you and Owen could meet me at my house. I'll feed you. You can stay the night and be on the road in the morning."

When Evie hesitated again, he added. "I know you are eager to get moving. I understand."

As he and Owen started to walk back to the pizza shop to get the car, Evie said, "Thank you. I won't forget this."

"Just let me know when you and Owen are safe."

Evie started to say, "I will," but instead walked over to the man and hugged him. Stepping back, she added, "Rent one without a tracker in it."

The man nodded, "Smart. Will do."

Owen smiled at the two of them, gave Evie a mock salute, and said, "I'll be back," in an awful imitation of the Terminator.

Evie waited until they had driven away and then walked back to her backpack, wondering if she was doing the right thing. It would be easy to leave now. Owen had someone who cared about him now. Did he really need to leave? Was it right to involve him in whatever was going on with her?

She walked a few feet into the woods and waited for an answer. All she heard was the singing of birds and a squirrel yelling at her from the tree.

She started walking.

FOURTEEN

"I was afraid you wouldn't be here when I got back."

"I wasn't. And now I am."

Owen looked at her and smiled before saying, "Shall we go?"

Owen drove, and Evie guided using the maps that The Pizza Shop owner had put in the car for them, along with a backpack and a sleeping bag for Owen, a tent, hiking boots, and a cooler with food in it. There was even a bag filled with snacks and more food bars.

"How did he do this? Why did he do this?" Evie had asked when they first got to the car.

"He asked for my shoe size."

"No, I mean all of this? How did he have time to pull all this together?"

"I asked him the same thing. He said he went into the camping store and said he was going camping and walked out with everything they told him to buy, including the maps. He got lots of different ones just in case someone asked, so no one would know where he was going."

"I'll never be able to thank him enough," Evie said, now an hour out of town. "And I never even asked his name."

Owen smiled, his eyes on the road. Evie thought that he might be only a teenager, but he was already wiser than most people she knew. Not that she remembered anybody, but it felt that way to her.

"His name is James Cahill. And he said to tell you that giving me a chance for an adventure was payment enough for him, and of course, letting him know when we get where we are going and are safe.

"Speaking of which, where are we going exactly. And why? And how will we know when we are safe? Because you know, don't you, that you haven't told me a single thing about why you are out walking and are so afraid."

Evie looked out at the scenery. They were heading east towards Boise, Idaho. She had found a place near there for them to camp for the night.

"It's beautiful here," she said. "I wonder if I have ever seen this before."

"You don't know?"

"I don't, which is why I haven't told you anything. I woke up yesterday in my sleeping bag, with no memory of who I am or why I was there. Only a sense of danger, and that I was hiding from someone. That's it. Nothing else. Except for a slip of paper in my hat that has an address in Doveland, Pennsylvania."

Owen started laughing. He slapped the steering wheel with his palm.

"Now, I get it. Why your name sounds so familiar. You named yourself last night!"

Evie pointed her finger at him and said, "Bingo! It seemed like those men were being brave and were becoming themselves, which is exactly what I am trying to do. So why not?

"And now that I have met you, Owen, I see you are the same. I haven't said thank you properly yet, for you and your friend, James. I hope I haven't gotten you into too much danger."

Owen shook his head and, for a moment, glanced over at Evie before turning his eyes back to the road.

"No, you haven't put me in danger. Instead, it's me thanking you for taking me with you and for helping me to be brave and become myself."

He paused and, with a hitch in his voice, added, "And for seeing me."

Evie reached over and patted his leg. "It's you and me then. You're my brother. Our last names are different because I was married."

Owen nodded, tears his eyes. "You got it, sis!"

• • • • ● • ● • • •

It only took a few hours of driving and stopping at places to show Alice's picture before Ace realized that he would never find her that way. When people asked why he was looking for her, he would say that she had gone missing, and although the police were looking, he couldn't sit, hope, and wait.

Some people were nice enough. They looked and said, "No." Others grunted and said perhaps she wanted to be missing. One woman at a gas station had put her hand on his arm, and looking up into Ace's eyes, said, "Honey, if you are meant to be together, nothing can keep you apart."

He gave her his best smile and said thank you, while at the same time wanting to snarl and throw things. What a bunch of drivel. Even if that were true, that wouldn't work in his case.

Later, as he drove, Ace wondered if it wasn't true. Maybe it didn't just mean that soul-mate love crap. Perhaps it also applied to other things, like karma from past lives. He had read about that. You gotta make up for past life stuff.

Ace didn't believe a word of that either, but what could it hurt to pretend that he did. And since he had no other options and was looking for a needle in a massive haystack, he might as well head to Pennsylvania and hope that he got some kind of sign once he got there. He texted Leo that he was on the road and had a lead. He would let him know when he found her.

He didn't say "if he found her." He had to make Leo think that he knew what he was doing. Even if he didn't. Ace realized that there was some irony in what was happening. Alice was hiding from him and her father. But Ace was also hiding from her father—both of them fugitives from the same man.

The difference was, once he found her and turned her over to her dad, she would probably not survive it. On the other hand, he might not either. Maybe they weren't so different after all.

Ace pulled off into the parking lot of a pizza shop and took the sim card out of his phone. At the next used car dealership he found, he'd trade his car in for one made before they had tracking systems. He'd load up on cash before then. Leo might track him to the car dealership, but from there, he would disappear until he found Alice. Then he would decide what to do. Turn her over, or run with her. If she let him.

Doubtful, he told himself, *but it was an option.*

As Ace sat there, he realized he was starving, and since he had pulled into a pizza place, why not get some? His mouth watering, he strode to the door only to find a sign that said. "Gone camping for a week. While I'm gone, try Frank's Pizza, a mile east of here. It's almost as good."

Someone had drawn a happy face on the sign with the words, "I'll be back."

Ace felt like ripping the sign off the door. He wouldn't be back. But he would try Frank's pizza. Why not? One pizza place was the same as another.

FIFTEEN

After dinner, everyone moved to the living room to listen to Thomas. They each chose their favorite place to sit, after first offering Thomas a comfortable chair and putting a cup of coffee for him on the table beside the chair. Ava thought back on the many stories that had unfolded in that living room. They had designed the house in anticipation that people would gather there to provide support. Not just for each other, but for anyone else who came to them for help.

But their first gathering had not been in Doveland. It had been in Sandpoint, Idaho. She had been living there with her mother's friend Suzanne after her mother died. Leif and Sarah had been living quiet lives in Sandpoint when Mira called asking for help. That was the beginning. Mira had found her twin brother Tom, and as more people became involved, all of them found that they belonged together. They were a karass.

The minute she and Evan met, they knew they were meant to be together. Sarah had suggested they take time for themselves, so they spent almost a year traveling until they found Doveland.

Since then, one by one, everyone had moved to Doveland. And although some of the karass had gone to another dimension—including Sarah, Leif, and Ava's daughter

Hannah—and others had moved away, they knew that changed nothing. They would always be a karass. They would always welcome those that needed help: people who had stories to tell and secrets to share.

And it was in their living room where people told many of their stories and revealed their secrets. Some stories involved a mystery. Some of those mysteries took longer to solve. Some had been dangerous to the entire karass.

But they had always helped. And they all had one outcome in common, Ava realized. Loved ones found each other again.

This was why she wasn't surprised that Thomas needed help to prepare for a granddaughter he never met. But even though that was the story he told, everyone listening knew it was more than physical help that he needed. Yes, they could provide that kind of service. But even though Thomas might not be aware of it, there was more going on than appeared on the surface, and they could provide that kind of help too.

As Thomas told his story, his heart felt lighter and lighter. It was as if the people in the living room were lifting something off of him. Not just the problem of getting his house ready for Alice, but something else.

He looked over at Grace, and she smiled at him. He knew she was the one who would tell him more about what this group did. They looked ordinary, but he was realizing that they weren't that at all.

By the time the night was over, they had arranged everything. Hank would handle all the work structure of his house. Grace would come over in the morning to survey the garden and make plans for its renewal.

Valerie would come with her, and after looking at the interior of his home, would give him suggestions to bring it up to the present, not locked in the past.

By then, Thomas had felt as if he had lived ten years in one day and was grateful that Hank had been wise enough to drive instead of him. He hated driving in the dark, anyway.

Everyone stood and hugged him, each hug feeling as if it was feeding him. He might have felt more tired than he had for years, but he also felt younger.

The last person to hug him was Johnny. Everyone else had turned away, on purpose or not, Thomas wasn't sure. But it gave Johnny a chance to whisper to him, "She's safe and on her way."

Johnny patted Thomas on the hand, smiled, winked, and turned away.

As Hank helped Thomas into his seatbelt, Thomas asked, "Who are these people?"

Hank did the same thing as Johnny. Smiled and winked. And then, with a catch in his throat, said, "My family. And now yours if you wish."

· · · ● · ● · · ·

Although they had warned Thomas that they would start early, it startled him to hear his doorbell ring at 6 a.m., and what sounded like an army of trucks coming down the street.

Carefully getting out of bed despite the noise—he had fallen more than once in the past when he forgot to make sure his feet were firmly planted on the ground—he made his way to the door.

Opening it, he found a smiling Hank and a group of men right behind him, armed with a variety of tools. Some tools looked vaguely familiar. Most did not. A truck was unloading a dumpster in the yard, and men were pulling ladders off another truck. Speechless, he just stood there until Hank touched him on the shoulder and guided him into the house.

"I'll make coffee, Thomas, while you take a shower, because the water is going off soon."

Still too stunned to say anything, Thomas started down the hallway to the bathroom, turned around, and came back. Hank was staring at his coffee pot.

"Tommy," Thomas said. "My friends call me Tommy."

Hank smiled as Tommy walked away and then turned back to the coffeepot. This was the first thing that had to go.

He called Grace, asked her to bring some good coffee for him and the men, and then started taking things out of the cupboards and putting them onto the counter.

Tommy would need to choose what he wanted to keep because the cabinets would be gone by the end of the day.

As Hank stood there thinking of the chaos they would create, he realized that this was not the place for Tommy to stay.

Hank made another phone call. He knew Ava would say yes, that's what the bunkhouse was for. Besides, they had turned their home into a bed-and-breakfast a few years before. They were picky about who stayed there, but he knew Thomas—Tommy—would be welcome.

Besides, that way someone would watch over Tommy all the time. If Tommy's daughter Alice showed up in the meantime, the crew would know what to tell her.

When Grace showed up with coffee, she had Johnny with her.

Hank smiled. Johnny was one of their success stories. Just a few years before, Johnny had started hanging out with the wrong crowd, but now he was a member of the Stone Circle, with gifts that hadn't yet been fully developed, but the ones he had were impressive.

Plus, he was a darn good worker and was the unspoken leader of the youth group he and Pete managed.

Hank knew there was more than one reason Johnny had shown up to help. But he would have to wait to find out what it was.

SIXTEEN

L eo felt like throwing his phone across the room. Ace wasn't answering his phone. Now he was sure. He had made a mistake in trusting Ace to watch over his daughter. Ace had promised he wouldn't fall for Alice, that his loyalties would always lie with Leo. But he should have known better. His daughter was beautiful. Smart. Capable. Witty. And kind. Everything that any normal father would want in a daughter. He should be proud.

Instead, he was ... what was he? Leo asked himself. *He was angry and disappointed.* There was no way he was going to admit he was also afraid. Afraid that the qualities his daughter had and her code of ethics would outsmart him. It would never happen. It wasn't what should have happened between him and Alice, but if he was going to be honest, at least with himself, it was his fault.

When Alice was young, when he had bothered to come home, they had some good times together. She called him daddy and would run after him when he went away for business trips. Sometimes when he was away, he missed her and would call her and her mother when she was still alive. But mostly, he didn't. He had been afraid even then of Alice, that she would discover who he was, and not love him. So he tried not to love her. Succeeded, mostly.

After Maggie died, Alice became even more clingy. She cried and cried when he left her with the woman he had hired to stay with her when he was away. At first, he liked Alice's need for him. No one had so openly loved him before, not even Maggie.

Maggie was broken before he met her. Too many drugs. Too much wild living. But he liked that about her. She was easy to control, and they had a passionate relationship that he had hoped would satisfy him for years.

But then Maggie had gotten pregnant. By mistake, she claimed. He doubted it because before Maggie got pregnant, she had worked hard at getting clean. No more drugs. No more drinking. As Maggie's head cleared, her passion for him faded. At first, it didn't matter. He could find what he needed elsewhere as long as she loved him. And didn't ask questions, which she started to do.

He thought that she loved him, so to be a good husband, he stayed home from business trips as her due date came closer so he could be present at Alice's birth. Although he wasn't fond of the name Alice, he had given into Maggie's desire to call her Alice after she explained she wanted their daughter to have a magical life.

He had almost cried when the nurse put Alice in his arms. She was so little and so helpless. He bent over to kiss her, thinking that she had chosen the right father because he was the one who could provide that magical life for her.

The next few years were happy for all of them. Family trips. Butterfly kisses on his daughter's forehead at night when he tucked her in when he was home.

Either Maggie had been a brilliant actress, or she was genuinely happy those few years. She didn't seem to mind his long absences. She had Alice. She stayed away from drugs and drink.

Which was a good thing, and yet it was not. With a clear mind, Maggie noticed more things. She started asking more questions.- Leo knew that Maggie loved him, but she was breaking the rules. Do not ask questions. Her questions were easier to answer in the beginning, and he did it, thinking that would be enough. He ran a referral business. No, it couldn't be found anywhere because his clients were private. They didn't want others to know they had hired him. He only got work through referrals.

At first, that made sense to Maggie. Leo knew that she loved the lifestyle he had made for her and Alice. Alice had anything she wanted. He thought that giving her the magic that she asked for was enough. But the questions continued. To make it worse, Maggie started resenting that he kept her and Alice isolated. She mentioned having friends and maybe getting a car of her own.

That's when he knew that eventually he would have to do something about her. He couldn't afford a curious wife. And the day he found her packing to go home to her father, well, that was the day he knew she had found out what kind of business he really did.

As Alice grew up, she became less clingy and more resigned to him not being around. She slowly withdrew from him, and he was glad. The housekeeper told him that Alice had nightmares long into her teen years. She would wake up and call for her mother.

Hearing that, he stayed away from home even more, just in case. Because Leo had lucked out. Although Alice remembered the accident, she was missing the part of the memory where he had deliberately driven into the lake, shoving Maggie's head against the car door as he did so. Hard enough that she passed out before hitting the water.

Alice did remember him rescuing her, and although he had shielded her eyes, he had always been a little afraid that she had seen him not try to save her mother. In fact, he had given Maggie one last push against the car door just to make sure she didn't wake up in time. That was sloppy of him, he knew, but it had to be done.

However, it was worse than that. In his anxiety to stop Maggie from leaving, he had never looked at the plane tickets. He didn't know where she was going, and they never found the tickets in the lake. So he hired people to research where she was going, but she had been much smarter than he had thought. She had booked five flights—all to different parts of the country. At the time, he decided it didn't matter. She was dead, and his secrets were buried with her.

Except, now Leo knew that Alice knew what her mother had found out. He had to find her.

SEVENTEEN

James had actually planned to go camping for a week. When he bought gear for Owen and Evie, he had bought the same for himself. Closing The Pizza Shop for the week was not a hardship. He only kept it going because it gave him something to do. When he still had a wife and a son and daughter, he had promised them repeatedly that he would go on trips with them. Yes, they would go camping. Yes, he promised—every year.

And never did. Instead, he had been busy making money. And drinking and partying with his friends after work when he should have gone home. Later, after he stopped drinking, he realized he had been what people called a mean drunk. Didn't know it at the time. He probably wouldn't have cared if he had.

Even after his wife left him, taking the kids with her, he still drank. Worse probably, since he no longer had to make up reasons why he didn't come home. Then one night, he almost ran over a person walking by the side of the road. He missed them, but not by much. And the look of terror on their face had scared him senseless. Finally.

And now here he was, camping by himself. How stupid is this, he asked himself. He was lying in his sleeping bag, in a tent, at a camping site near town. He hadn't had time to get far before night fell. He had struggled through putting up the tent, helped by a man walking by who had a tent set up at the next site. He pulled in his sleeping bag, and tried to sleep.

All he could think about was what was missing. His wife and kids. Family. Adventure. Finally, he fell asleep for a few hours. When he woke up, he walked over to the man's campsite and told him he realized he wasn't a camper. Could his family use an extra tent and sleeping bag? In fact, could they use all the supplies he bought? Brand new.

The man's wife came out to stand beside him, smiling at the strange man in front of her. What did she see, he wondered?

Through the open flap of the tent, James could see three children snuggled together under blankets.

"Do any of you have sleeping bags?" he asked.

"We get by," the man answered.

"Well, I have more money than I'll ever need, and if you let me buy you all what you need, you will have filled my heart for the day. Please."

Seeing the two look at each other, wondering if the man in front of them was crazy, he added, "Please. You have no idea how much it would mean to me to get you what you need. Please."

The woman looked up at her husband, and he nodded.

"Thank you," she said, and asked, "May I hug you?"

"Group hug?" he asked.

She nodded and called the kids to come out and say thank you to this nice man. Afterward, they helped him pack up his camping gear and put it into their car and followed him into town, where he bought them the rest of their supplies, adding things they hadn't asked for when they weren't looking.

Out in the parking lot, he hugged them all one last time and then slipped an envelope into the woman's hand filled with cash.

"For the kids," he said and walked away.

71

He waited in his car until he saw them drive safely away and then made two phone calls. One was to a man who had been trying to buy The Pizza Shop for years. He told him to get a lawyer to draw up the papers. He quoted him a price far below what they had initially agreed upon, which included the car that said "The Pizza Shop" on it. He would mail him the keys.

After a moment's silence, the man said, "I don't know why you are doing this, but thank you."

James knew the man had a wife and kids. They would enjoy having the shop. The thought of it lightened his heart even more.

The next call James made was to a realtor he had known for years from Toastmasters. This call took longer. There were many more things to plan. Someone would need to pack his house because he wanted to sell it. Have them throw away or give away everything that wasn't obviously personal, like picture albums.

Pack that stuff away and store it for him. He'd pay them to do all that for him. It shouldn't be much. Once he knew where he was going, he'd have the boxes shipped.

He could do everything else by phone and email. To the question of why, James just said he was ready to have an adventure. Said it was a delayed mid-life crisis. His friend laughed and said he wished he could join him.

James paused before answering and then told him that perhaps he should think about what he wanted in life. It had taken him a long time to realize what that was for him.

"Don't wait too long," James told his friend.

After the last phone call, James Cahill sat in his car and thought through his next move. He could go anywhere in the world. He could sell his car and get on a plane. Have the adventures in Europe his wife had wanted. He played with the idea for a while and then turned the key and started the engine. He could do that. But that's not what he really wanted. He wanted to see Owen and Evie again. They were headed to Pennsylvania. He would too.

He had a feeling that was where the adventure would be, and he wanted to be part of whatever was happening. Besides, he needed them to be safe. Yes, he knew he was substituting them for the kids he had lost, but for now, it was what he had, and he was grateful to have a purpose. It had been missing for a long time. In fact, he wasn't sure he ever had one. Now he did.

EIGHTEEN

Johnny watched his mother and Craig maneuver gracefully around each other in the kitchen and smiled to himself. He missed his father and had not wanted him to die. But if he was thinking logically, which he tried to do most of the time, Johnny knew it had been the best solution.

And since he was well aware that people didn't vanish forever, that they lived on, just in different places, he knew that someday he would see his father again. That his father had died was a good thing. Dealing with his father would have been difficult for both him and his mother because she would not have found the happiness she had now.

The release from Harold's influence after the arrival of Ava's group to Doveland had changed everything for the better for them. It was because of them he had not followed his father into evil ways. Johnny had made one mistake and learned from it.

Then he discovered he had extra gifts, as his mother called them, and realized that from then on he had to always watch his motives before taking any action. He couldn't let himself be led astray and cause damage to anyone in any way.

Craig turned and noticed Johnny staring at his cereal, slid a piece of toast made just the way he liked it under his nose, and asked, "Everything all right?"

One thing Johnny had promised himself is that he would always tell the truth. Or try to. He had seen too much evil happen because people lied to themselves first and then to others.

So he glanced up at Craig, then looked at Johnny's younger brother Lex sitting across from him at the table, and then finally at his mother before answering, "Yes. And things are coming that will change our lives."

Craig and Johnny's mom looked at each other and then sat down at the table. It was his mom who asked, "Is it dangerous? Is there anything we can do about it, now?"

"It's about Thomas, isn't it?" Craig asked.

"Tommy," Lex popped in, shoving a piece of toast into his mouth at the same time. "I heard that his friends call him Tommy."

"When did you first hear that?" Valerie asked.

"At his house, when he was talking to Hank."

"And when was this?"

Lex put down his toast, realizing he had probably said something he shouldn't have. But he liked Tommy. He had wanted to see where he lived, so he had visited.

"Yesterday morning, really early," he mumbled.

Craig, Valerie, and Johnny looked at each other and back to Lex.

"But you were here, Lex," Craig said.

"What is it with this place?" Valerie huffed. "Is it the water?"

Craig laughed.

"It's probably that the idea that there are other ways to move around, to see, to experience life, has become part of the fabric of Doveland.

"Lex has been around it for years. It probably never occurred to him he couldn't do what he did."

"What did I do?" Lex asked.

"What do you think you did?" Johnny asked, smiling at his little brother, who wasn't so little anymore.

"I wanted to see the new guys' house, so I visited it in my mind. Like what some of your friends do. Like Mira and Tom. It's how they found each other, even though they were adopted by different families. You know. Remember?"

Valarie stood and smiled.

"I remember. But now it's time for school, and you'll miss the bus. Let's go." She paused and then added, "And this is a conversation we will have to have because you can't just go popping into people's homes without them knowing about it."

"But..." Lex started to say, and his mother cut him off.

"No buts about it. They can't see you, so they don't know you are there. It's rude, and it's wrong. I know that you didn't know. But now you do. You need permission, and you need to let them know you are there."

"But ...," Lex tried to say again, but this time Johnny stopped him.

"Lex. Mom's right. We'll talk about it later."

Lex got up, grabbed his jacket, was almost out the door before he turned around and tried one more time.

"But ..."

This time it was Craig's shake of the head that stopped him. So Lex continued the conversation with himself.

"But I saw something else that you might want to know about."

Then the bus honked, and Lex went flying out the door, leaving behind three worried people.

In school, Lex high-fived his friends and slid into his seat in history class. School was hard for him. He hated having to sit still for so long. And the subjects were boring. What did it have to do with real life? It was this feeling that he had been missing out on things that had started him wandering in his mind outside of the building.

Daydreaming again? A teacher would ask when he didn't hear the question. But after his parents and Johnny's reaction, he realized that somewhere along the way it had changed to more than daydreaming. He had started imagining himself in places. And now he realized it had moved from imagining he was there to being there.

Yes, he had seen Thomas tell Hank to call him Tommy. He hadn't imagined it. Lex missed everything the teacher said after that. If he hadn't imagined it, then it meant that perhaps he could go anywhere, and he needed to talk to someone who knew what to do about that.

And if he hadn't imagined it, then it was true. People were heading to Doveland, and he needed to tell someone. Maybe it was Tommy's daughter. But her name wasn't Alice. And she had someone with her. But it wasn't only her. There were other people coming too. One of them was really mad.

"Lex!" His teacher shouted from the front of the room. "Don't make me ask you again. What is the answer to the question?"

A piece of paper slid in front of him, and he said what was on it.

The teacher huffed and turned away, mumbling, "Right."

Lex looked at his friend and said, "Thanks!"

His friend said, "What are friends for?"

And brothers, Lex thought. *I need to talk to Johnny.*

NINETEEN

On the way to the campground, Evie and Owen drove through a McDonald's and got dinner. Neither one of them felt like doing anything other than sleeping.

They pitched the tent together with the idea that they both would sleep in there. However, after seeing how cramped the tent was, Evie said she'd sleep in the back of the car with the liftgate open. She'd be more comfortable there, she assured Owen.

Owen agreed but moved the car, so it was parked directly in front of the tent. Once she was safely inside the car, he climbed into the tent but left the flap open.

"You don't need to do that, you know," Evie had said, poking her head up from her sleeping bag. "I am perfectly safe."

"Sure, I know. This way, you can protect me."

They both laughed, knowing it really was the other way around. Before Evie fell asleep, she wondered if anyone had ever tried to protect her before. The answer that came to her was that her mother had. But it was a fleeting memory, like a wisp of a dream drifting in the wind.

A mother, Evie thought. *Of course, I have a mother. Maybe that's where we are going. To my mother's.*

With that hope in her heart, Evie drifted off to sleep. And dreamed. And screamed.

Owen woke up and screamed too. Terrified that something had happened to Evie, he scrambled out of his bag and out of the tent, only to see Evie still sleeping, obviously having a nightmare.

Not knowing whether he should wake her, he stood at the car. A few flashlights beamed his way, and a man called out if everything was alright.

Owen ran over to him and whispered, "It's okay. My sister is having a nightmare."

The man looked Owen over—with his sweatpants, t-shirt, brown hair uncombed—smiled, relaxed, and turned off his flashlight.

"Does your sister have these nightmares often?"

Owen truthfully answered, "I don't know."

Seeing the man squint at him, Owen added, "I was away at school and haven't seen her for a while. We decided to camp together to get to know each other again."

After answering, "Everything is okay," to other people calling out, Owen thanked the man for his concern and headed back to the car.

He could feel the man staring at him as he walked. It made him nervous, but he did his best to walk normally. The way anyone would walk going back to a sister having a nightmare.

Owen found Evie sitting up in her bag, leaning forward so her head wouldn't hit the ceiling. Owen had the fleeting thought that it was good that Evie was so much shorter than him. He could never have sat up comfortably in the back of the car.

"You okay?"

"I had a nightmare."

"Yeah. That was obvious. Woke up the entire campground."

"Oh, God," Evie said, burying her face in her hands. "I'm sorry."

"Want to talk about it?"

Evie looked at the young boy standing in front of her, concern written all over his face, and wondered how she had ever decided to befriend this person. She had a feeling she had never made friends before. It worried her. Why not? Had she always been afraid? Not just now? Always?

And that brought back the nightmare. It felt familiar. Was her memory returning? If nightmares were part of her life, did she want to remember?

"I don't remember much, really. Something about water."

Owen said out loud what she had been thinking.

"Maybe this is a good thing. Maybe your memory is coming back?"

"Maybe."

She turned to lie back down as Owen headed into the tent and then turned around.

"Owen, did you sleep enough? Something is freaking me out here. Can we go now?"

Although he was sure they had only slept a few hours, Owen was happy to leave. Something was bothering him too, but he couldn't figure out what it was. He was used to sleeping in strange places. The Pizza Shop was never comfortable, but it always felt safe. This didn't.

He looked around and saw nothing but the lights on around the campground's buildings. Everyone else had gone back into their tents.

"Absolutely," he said. "Let's go."

· · · · ● · ● · · ·

What neither Owen nor Evie saw was the man who had been watching them talk together, check his phone and then duck inside his tent. He started rolling up his sleeping bag and putting the few things he had with him into his pack.

It was pure dumb luck that he had seen them. He had gotten a text a few days before with the girls' picture.

"Text this number if you see this girl," it had said.

He got stuff like that all the time, so he had ignored it. What were the chances he would camp out in the same place where the girl in the picture had stopped?

And if she hadn't screamed and woken up the entire campground, he never would have seen her.

"Where?" the text read.

"Outside Boise," he answered.

"Follow her," it said.

The man stepped outside, thinking now that everything had settled down, he could put a tracker on her car.

"Missed them. They're gone."

"They?"

"She's with a boy."

"Idiot. That's not her."

The man unrolled his bag and lay back down, thinking that the person on the other phone was the idiot. It was the girl. But it meant nothing to him.

He rolled over to go back to sleep, thinking that if they were running from the idiot on the other end, he figured they would be safe for a little longer. He hoped they would be. They seemed like nice enough kids.

TWENTY

Ava took Thomas—"Tommy, please,"— to the bunkhouse. He had packed a small bag with Hank's help, and although Hank said he would drive him, Thomas said it wasn't far, and he wanted to be able to get around on his own if he needed to. He wasn't that much older than Hank. Besides, he wanted to keep checking on his house.

Hank had laughed, realizing how true that was, and said he would see him later that night. Thomas had driven off, taking one last look at his house that now looked as if an army of ants had swallowed it.

Has it been only a day since I decided to come back to the land of the living? he asked himself.

When Hank had told Thomas that he could stay at the bunkhouse, he had said yes, thinking he would be staying someplace rustic and probably not very comfortable.

But as he and Ava had walked the gravel path to the bunkhouse, he realized that he had it all wrong. There was nothing rustic about it.

Inside, it looked just like the inside of the main house, except smaller. A large open space held couches and a TV and a mini kitchen. Around the space were doors, which Tommy realized led to the individual rooms.

All the doors were open except one, which Ava pointed to and said that was Hank's. It was permanently his, so he could stay in Doveland anytime he wished to. Hank had a small farm and home in Concourse left to him a few years before by a man named Melvin Byler.

Did Tommy know him? Thomas shook his head, both answering no to Ava's question and also in amazement at the room Ava had taken him to.

It wasn't big, but it looked so comfortable he wanted to drop on the bed and take a nap. Before leaving him there, Ava showed him a large closet where he could keep his things, a small desk for working, and his bathroom.

"Wait," he said. "I thought this was a bunkhouse. I was expecting a common bathroom."

Ava laughed, "Well, we have that too for a few of the rooms, but of course, as our special guest, we wanted you to have one of the rooms with a bathroom. It's only a shower, but there is a jacuzzi around the side if you like that kind of thing."

"Never had one," Thomas said, wondering again how much he had missed out on by closing his life off after losing his wife, then his daughter, and then when no longer needed at his job.

"Well, it's about time you try it," Ava said. "I'll leave you here to get set up. You are welcome to join us for our meals or make your own. Of course, you can probably tell, we are often hosting a group of friends, and then I do hope you will choose to join us."

Thomas put his bag down and turned to Ava, "I don't understand how all this happened. And so quickly. One minute I was a hermit, and the next, I am part of a community. I don't know how I will ever be able to thank you."

"No, need, Tommy. Just pass it on when the time is right. In the meantime, let yourself be excited that your granddaughter is on her way."

Thomas nodded. Ava reached over and hugged him and then closed the door behind her.

As she walked back to the house, she thought about how many people they had hosted at the bunkhouse and how often it was because there was more going on than appeared on the surface. She was sure that was true this time, too.

There was a reason Thomas had come to them. Even though he didn't know it yet, he was now with a group of people who had what many people called magical skills. But they knew that it wasn't magic at all. Only gifts that allowed them to see more of what was going on than most people could see.

She was not one of those people who could remote-view or astral-project. She didn't even read thoughts the way that others could. But she could feel when things were right and when things were not. And there was definitely something going on with Thomas' granddaughter.

It wasn't just the granddaughter. It was what she was bringing. Yes, some of it was good. But some of it wasn't. It felt familiar. They had dealt with this kind of thing before. The forces that didn't want people to know that there is much more to life than what appears as a physical world. She knew the forces and the people they controlled loved power and money, and didn't care how they got it.

Yes, Ava had experience with these people. People who hated anyone who they thought could stop them from getting what they wanted. They hated people with the kinds of gifts she and her friends had and who could clearly see the evil they were doing. If Thomas' granddaughter was bringing people like that to Doveland, they needed to be prepared.

Ava paused in Ben's bedroom and watched him sleep. He always claimed that he was too old to take naps, but he still did anyway. Short ones, maybe, but still. She missed her daughter, Hannah. But when Hannah returned to Erda, Ava had known it was the right thing to do and supported her decision. She couldn't have stopped her, anyway. Still, in her heart, she missed her, and in her honor, sewed ladybugs onto Ben's clothes just as she had done on Hannah's.

Ava knew that couldn't be forever. When Ben started school, he would probably tell her to stop. On the other hand, the world was changing. Maybe he would be okay with it because he knew what it meant—that he was loved.

As Ava prepared lunch, she realized that was what Thomas had been missing. The knowledge that he was loved. He had been, she knew, but he thought that it was missing. Now the granddaughter he never knew was coming to him, and Thomas hoped that his granddaughter was bringing love.

That she is, Ava thought. *But she is also afraid, and she has a right to be.*

Ben yelled that he was up, and Ava's attention turned to his care. But the feeling that both something good and something evil was coming their way remained with her.

TWENTY ONE

He mumbled to himself as he drove. Ace told himself that he was crazy. Why was he headed to Pennsylvania? How was he going to find Alice? He knew nothing more than that she was from there. He didn't know if she would go back. He knew nothing. Nothing except Leo would now be like a rabid dog, foaming at the mouth, panting with anger, all directed at him.

Which made it even stupider to be going some place looking for Alice. He should be running. Maybe drive up into Canada and then take a flight out of there to some remote island. Someplace Leo would never find him. Someplace where he could change his name, and find a nice ordinary girl, settle down like normal people. Maybe have a kid or two. Teach them to play baseball. Or football.

Ace's imagination took over. He could see himself tossing the ball to boys who looked just like him, with a touch of their mother. She wouldn't be too pretty so as not to call attention to herself, but she would be a wonderful mother and a kind wife. What more could he want? As he pictured the scene, he saw a young girl standing beside one of the boys, and he smiled at her.

Did she want to play catch too? "No, daddy," she said, "I want you to come home."

That voice was so real in his head that Ace almost swerved off the road. He didn't have a daughter. He didn't have a wife, sons, or a normal life. He was an errand boy, one who did the dirty work for men like Leo. Well, only Leo, after Leo hired him to be Alice's boyfriend. He had warned him what would happen if he didn't make sure that Alice wasn't a danger to him.

"To her father?" Ace had asked Leo.

Leo had reached out and slapped Ace across the face. So hard, he had fallen to his knees. His first instinct had been to get up and start fighting, but he was at least wise enough to know that he would lose, so he had stayed down until Leo put his hand down and helped him stand.

"Never question me again," he had said, his face inches away. So close that Ace could smell the hint of garlic on his breath and something else that made his stomach turn. So close that he could see the yellow flecks in Leo's green eyes. So close that when Leo spoke, little drops of spit landed on Ace's face.

Ace pulled off at the next exit and into the nearest fast food restaurant. He had started shaking so hard he wasn't sure he could drive. The memory of Leo burned into his head, but also the memory of a little girl calling him to come home. Two different worlds. But he knew that he had already agreed to Leo's world, and a little girl who loved him would never be part of that.

So if that was true, what was he doing? Yes, perhaps he thought that if he found Alice, he would call Leo and tell him, and free himself from Leo. Tell him where Alice was and then run. Run so far away that Leo could never find him. It was stupid to think these things, he told himself.

He knew it was a pipe dream. Leo's business guaranteed him that he had contacts everywhere. However, Ace didn't want to stop believing that it was possible. He had heard that anything was possible. Why not for him? Otherwise, he might as well call up Leo now and tell him to come shoot him.

On the other hand, that would not be a good idea because Leo wouldn't shoot him. That would be too easy. No, if he wanted a swift death, he would have to do it to himself. But he wasn't there yet.

Perhaps all this fantasy thinking is because I'm hungry, Ace thought. *I might as well get food while I am here.*

He had managed to pull into a McDonald's, and he knew their french fries were ready at 10:30. He glanced at his watch. A regular watch. Not on line. He wasn't that stupid. And saw that it had just turned 10:30. His mouth watered and he felt better already just thinking about the fries. Fat, sugar, salt, all in one. Just what he needed.

Ace watched the girl behind the counter react to him. It helped his state of mind. He still had it. No, he wasn't all that good looking. Short by most standards, but that worked in his favor with Alice since she was so tiny.

His hair was a little too long, not having time to get it cut after Alice went missing. So he had smoothed his dark blond hair back with water in the bathroom, did a quick shave in the sink, and felt better.

Most of his life he had spent outside, so he had squint lines around his brown eyes, but he knew that didn't hurt him, either. But what really helped him was the combination of softness and hardness and good manners that he had with only a hint that danger lay beneath it.

He smiled at himself in the mirror, happy with what he saw. And then he smiled at the girl behind the counter the same way as she counted his money. Yes, he still had it.

Twenty minutes later, fortified by food, the attention of a pretty young thing, and coffee to go, Ace pulled back onto the I80 heading east. He wondered if he could drive straight through, or since he'd never get this way again, maybe he should see part of the country he had never seen before. Like the Corn Palace in

Mitchell, South Dakota, or the Jolly Green Giant statue in Blue Earth, Minnesota.

Are you crazy? He asked himself. *Where did these stupid ideas come from, anyway? He'd drive straight through, pull off and nap if necessary, but get to Pennsylvania.*

He'd worry about where to go once he got there. Maybe as he got closer, he would remember something else that Alice had said that would help him figure out where to go.

It was a plan. Good or bad, it almost didn't matter. It gave him something to do. Stupid or not. He was doing it.

TWENTY TWO

As Ace pulled out of the parking lot, he almost ran into another car. Yes, he was pulling out of the entrance, but still, it wasn't his fault. He glanced over at the car and noticed the man looking at him with a shocked look on his face.

"Idiot," Ace had said as he showed him his middle finger.

The man didn't react, just stared.

"Idiot," Ace mumbled to himself again, even though he recognized he might have also been talking to himself.

What Ace didn't know was the man in the blue SUV had a shocked look, not only because he had almost been hit by another car, but because the moment the man looked over at him, he thought he saw someone sitting beside him.

But after the man had given him the finger, he realized there was no one in the car but some guy with slicked-back dark blond hair, holding a soda cup in one hand and steering with the other—when he wasn't flipping him off.

James Cahill shook his head. Yes, in the past, he would have reacted with anger, just like that young man. But he had mellowed through the years. No longer young, never that good looking, he had accepted his life. Well, until yesterday. Now he was on the search for Owen and Evie, following them to somewhere in

Pennsylvania. He wasn't worried about finding them. Somehow it would work out. They would call, or he would know. It was interesting being this sure about something so intangible, but James liked the feeling.

At the counter, the girl was still lost in the vision of the last customer. So her smile to the short, stocky, and balding man in front of her was broader than usual.

"Where are you heading to?" She asked.

"To Pennsylvania," the man answered. His voice warm and his smile kind.

"Weird, that," she said, handing the man his change. "The man right before you was heading there too."

"Did he say where in Pennsylvania?"

"Nope. Said he didn't know yet. He'd decide. No, that's not what he said. He said he'd know when he got there."

James smiled at the girl and handed her back the change plus the two extra twenties in his hand. Behind him was a mother and her young son.

He leaned forward and said, "This is for them and you."

James quickly filled his cup with soda, grabbed the bag of french fries, and was out the door before the woman had finished ordering. He glanced up as he drove out and saw the woman looking out the window at him with a hand on her heart.

He smiled and waved and thought that perhaps that feeling would calm down the other one. The one he had felt when he learned that the man who had almost run into him was also heading to Pennsylvania.

Yes, it could be a coincidence, but he didn't think so. He had felt a bolt of fear run up his spine.

As amazing as it was, he was sure that they were heading to the same place, after the same person, but for entirely different reasons. However, James reasoned that he had something on his side. He knew about the man. He'd watch for him. The man didn't know about him.

He reached over and pulled out a french fry and smiled at the smell and the feel of salt on his fingers. It didn't take much to make him happy, he realized. It took a while to figure that out, but hey, he said to himself, better late than never.

• • • ● • ● • • •

The passenger in Ace's seat, the one James saw and then didn't see, the one that Ace didn't know was there, also said "Idiot." To Ace.

But Ace didn't hear him. Couldn't have heard him because the man wasn't actually there.

For a moment, the man felt that the man in the other car had glimpsed him. But that was impossible. He wasn't traveling in Ace's car. He was hundreds of miles away.

Only another remote viewer might have a chance of seeing him. And how many of them were there, anyway? But it reminded him that he had been lazy, not paying enough attention.

Still, he wanted to see where Ace was going, and now he knew. Pennsylvania. It made sense. But that didn't mean he had to like it. He hated Pennsylvania.

But of course, that had to be where the girl was going. Her grandfather lived there. And now he knew the town where everyone was heading to.

They might not know yet, but they would. However, since they were driving, he had the advantage. He'd wait a few days and fly into Pittsburgh, and get there in plenty of time.

It infuriated him that the girl had blocked him and was now cloaking both herself and that kid. How she was doing it having no memory was a mystery.

Instinct, he guessed. Yes, he should have made sure she died on that mountain. He wouldn't make that mistake a second time.

The man stood and walked to the large window that looked out over his favorite view. It was spectacular. He had homes all over the world but ended up here most of the time.

He loved it here on the top of this mountain, far from everyone and everything he controlled. That's what he had people for, but this situation called for his direct intervention.

He hated to leave, but he resigned himself to it since it looked like he would have to. He'd make the most of it. It was probably time for him to actually see people in person again. Isolated for too long, he might lose perspective. And maybe he could have a little fun too.

Turning away from the view, the man headed to his bedroom to pack.

He tapped his phone and heard, "Yes, Mr. Quinn."

"Get my car, I need to go to the airport."

He didn't wait for a response. Duke Quinn knew everyone jumped when he called. They had all felt his wrath. But no one knew him. And that was the way it had to remain.

That was why he had to stop that girl before everyone found out who he was and what he did to remain so rich and powerful.

TWENTY THREE

"Are we there yet?" Evie asked, rolling her neck to try to loosen it up.

She had not meant to fall asleep, but now that the sun appeared to be up, she realized that she had. Plus, her neck hurt.

Owen laughed. "What are you, ten?"

Evie laughed too, and then leaned back and said, "Seriously, where are we? How long have I been asleep?"

"On the I80 heading east and for hours."

Evie glanced at the car's clock and said, "More than a few hours. It's almost noon. Aren't you exhausted?"

"Hungry mostly."

Evie pointed to an exit sign that promised food, and without hesitation, Owen took the exit.

Fifteen minutes later, they were both dipping chips into salsa, waiting for their food to arrive. They smiled at each other. Anyone looking at them would never know they weren't just two ordinary people, probably siblings, having lunch together.

Once their food arrived, neither spoke, other than to make appreciative sounds and ask the server to fill their soda glasses.

"I had no idea I was so hungry," Owen said, putting down his spoon after the dish of fried ice cream that they were sharing was down to a melting slab."

"Me either," Evie answered. "Or so tired. Which means, Owen, you must be tired too. If you can drive for another couple of hours, I think we should stop at a motel and stay the night. Get cleaned up. Sleep."

"What about getting to Pennsylvania quickly? Aren't you running from something? Have you figured out what it is?"

Evie leaned back against the booth and closed her eyes.

"Yes. Yes. And not really. Yes, I want to get there quickly, but I want to get there safely, and I keep thinking that there is a timing to this. And right now, that timing says we are both too tired to deal with whatever I am running from.

"So yes, I am running from something. But I am also going towards—going towards something that is waiting for me to come. I am going towards whoever lives at this address. And the not really part is that I remember nothing concrete, but I have feelings about things now.

"That nightmare scared me, but it also seemed to open the door to some memories. Not memories, really. Impressions. Ideas."

Owen fingered his spoon, wondering if he should say anything, and decided that there was too much they didn't know to keep from sharing what they did.

"You know, back at the campsite when you got freaked out? Do you know why?"

"Just a feeling."

"Well, I had a weird feeling too about that man with the flashlight. He seemed normal and everything, but at the same time, I could have sworn he knew me. But since that is impossible, how could he?"

Evie glanced out the window. They were close enough to the highway that she could see the traffic streaming by.

All these people going somewhere. Where were they going? And why? Were they running or moving forward? Were any of them dangerous to her? All questions that had no answers.

Sighing, Evie said, "You know what? I don't remember anything about myself yet, but I do know that nothing is impossible. The only thing we can do right now is to follow the little breadcrumb of the address I found. I hope I am meant to go there and not stay away from it."

"Well, it must feel like 'go to it.' Otherwise, we wouldn't be going there, would we? Given our spidey senses and all that!" Owen said with a laugh.

"True that!" Evie said, slapping money on the table before heading out the door.

Owen looked at her and wondered to himself how a woman like that used the phrase "true that."

There was much more to Evie than appeared on the surface. He had known that the minute she walked into The Pizza Shop looking like roadkill and beautiful at the same time. Something told him to go with her, and here he was. He was going on an adventure.

Looking around the restaurant, he grabbed one last chip and followed Evie out the door. It seemed that was his purpose in life right now, follow his new sister, and get her where she was supposed to go.

A few hours later, they pulled into a motel in the middle of nowhere, as Evie requested. They had taken an exit and then driven a few miles further to find a motel, thinking it was safer not to take the first one.

Evie had given Owen cash from her roll of money, and he had gone to rent them a room with double beds when he saw a blue SUV pull into the motel's parking lot.

Staring, Owen knocked on Evie's window and pointed in the direction of the car. The driver had gotten out and was heading into the motel's lobby.

Evie stepped out of the car, and the two of them stared at the retreating figure.

"Is that who I think it is?" Evie asked.

Owen nodded. "Impossible, right?"

"Obviously not," Evie answered.

"Well, is it a good thing or not?"

Both of them stood still, thinking and then feeling. Then they looked at each other and started laughing.

"Good thing!" they said together and started running.

So when James Cahill came out of the door, head down, putting his money away, he didn't see the two of them running his way.

"Mr. Cahill," he heard instead, and looked up to see Owen and Evie heading towards him.

He was so startled he dropped his wallet, and it was Evie who picked it up and waited until Owen had finished hugging his ex-boss before handing it to him.

The three of them stood looking at each other with enormous smiles on their faces until James said, "Well, imagine that!"

Which started Owen and Evie laughing again.

"You're right, Evie," Owen said, "Nothing is impossible."

TWENTY FOUR

L ex stood outside of his brother's closed bedroom door, not
knowing what to do next. It was early morning, long before
anyone had to get up. Johnny was home, finishing up the last of his
classes for the semester online. Which meant he had probably been
up late studying and wouldn't appreciate a knock on his door so
early in the morning.

Perhaps he would just head downstairs and make a great
breakfast for his mom and brother. For the past few years, he had
been helping Alex at the Diner. Actually, Alex was teaching him
how to cook.

Watching Junior Chef had gotten him interested in learning,
and Alex and Pete, and even Sam when he was in town, had
volunteered to teach him. Between cooking and designing things,
Lex wasn't sure which one he liked best.

Which isn't the point right now, he told himself. Right now, he
thought perhaps he was having some kind of breakdown.

Yes, he knew that many people who lived in Doveland could do
things other people couldn't. Magical things. But they always told
him it wasn't magic, that it didn't make them special. It just gave
them more responsibility to use their gifts wisely.

All Lex could think was if it were a gift, he would like to return it to the store. There was nothing about it that made him happy or feel good. It just scared the pants off of him. And since his friend Hannah had gone to another dimension—as if that wasn't weird, and definitely not something he would ever tell anyone outside the Circle—he had no one his age to talk to.

When people asked where Hannah went, they were told she went to live with relatives. Why? They'd ask. What relatives? Why wasn't she on social media telling them what she was up to? Everyone mumbled answers, and eventually, people stopped asking.

Lex was reasonably sure that one of the Circle members had made everyone else forget about her because no one ever mentioned her anymore. For that, he was grateful. Yes, she went to live with relatives. That part was true. But that was about it. Everything else would sound like a fantasy.

As Lex made his way down the stairs, he paused on the landing and looked out over the town's park. One car drove around the traffic circle that enclosed the green and headed west to the lake. *Probably going fishing,* Lex thought.

A light flicked on in the coffeehouse, and he saw Grace walk past the window as she came down the stairs from her apartment. He'd been up there a few times. It was open and cozy at the same time. Just like Grace. Grace, who knew everybody and everything going on in Doveland.

Lex ran down the rest of the stairs, being careful not to make any noise. He slipped out the front door, remembering to lock the door behind him, and ran over to Your Second Home and tapped on the window. Knocking on the door wouldn't have done any good. They had built an entryway to keep the weather out, but it also kept out the sound of someone like him trying to get their attention.

He had heard that the windows were bulletproof. Something about all the danger that had followed the Circle when they had first moved to Doveland. Things had calmed down since then, at least in the outright danger department. But he was tapping on the window because of what he thought was heading to Doveland now.

Maybe bulletproof windows were a good idea, he thought. But the things he saw probably would not be stopped that way.

He knocked again and then saw Grace turn, smile, and head to the door to let him in. He stepped inside, grateful for the warmth. He had run out without a jacket, forgetting that it was still chilly this early in the morning.

Grace didn't ask why he was there as most people would. Instead, she ushered him over to a booth where no one could see them and asked if he would like something to eat.

There was no way he was going to turn that down, he thought. He loved to cook, but getting something to eat that he didn't make would be amazing. Grace had to have help with the cooking now that her business partner, Mandy, had moved away with her husband, Tom. But the scone Grace brought to him along with a hot chocolate was one she said she had made herself.

"I'd love to learn how to make these!" Lex said as he swallowed his first bite.

"I'd love to teach you," Grace replied. "And I hear that you have been turning into quite the cook at the Diner. If you want to try out pastries, come over anytime, and I, or one of my pastry chefs, will show you what we know."

Without thinking, Lex stood up and walked over to Grace's chair and hugged her around her neck. When he sat back down, he saw that she had tears in her eyes.

He looked down at his plate, embarrassed at what he had done. Grace reached over and held his hand.

"That was one of the sweetest hugs I have ever had. Thank you. Now, young man, you knocked on the window for a reason. I am ready to listen. I'll keep the doors locked until you have said everything you want to have said. And I will keep what you tell me to myself unless it is something you want me to share."

"That's your gift, isn't it," Lex said.

When Grace looked puzzled, he added, "Listening."

"I suppose it is. Is that what you want to tell me? Have you discovered a gift of your own, other than baking and designing? And let's add that you have the gift of wisdom because you knew enough to come to ask for help," she asked, her eyes twinkling.

"Someone is coming to Doveland who scares me."

"Do you know who it is?" Grace asked.

"Not his name. Not even much about what he looks like. Just what he feels like. Or what he is feeling."

Grace paused, knowing there was more.

"What else, Lex."

"I think he has seen me watching him."

TWENTY FIVE

Lex was right. The man he had been watching had felt his presence.

But, Leo had also felt someone watching him as he packed his bags. It worried him. He had felt this kind of thing before. Still, he kept packing. What else was he to do? He had to find Alice. And Ace.

The feeling he had was the same one he sometimes had when Maggie was alive. He'd be in a meeting somewhere, and he would feel her presence. Of course, she was never there. But she never asked where he had been or what his business was about. At first, he thought she didn't ask because she was too busy raising Alice to worry about where he was or what he was doing.

When he came home, she would make him feel like a king.

But the last few years before she died, her care-taking no longer felt natural. It felt forced. And Leo sensed her presence more often when he was away. It creeped him out.

Once, he asked her about it. He told her it felt like she was there in the room with him when he was away.

She had laughed and said, "Did you see me?"

And when he answered no, she laughed again and said it must have been his imagination. Maybe he imagined her being there because he missed her so much. And then she distracted him away from his worries by showing him what he had been missing.

Because months passed before he felt her presence again, he had accepted her explanation. But then it started happening again. And he started worrying that she was watching him and knew what he did with his time. It all came together for him. Somehow—he didn't know how—she had been spying on him. He had come home early from his assignment. He had completed his task and, as always, left town immediately. However, usually, he made a stop on the way home to have some fun. That time, he hadn't, which is how he caught her by surprise.

He had come directly home because he had felt Maggie's presence beside him as he slipped the poison into the man's drink. It would stop the man's heart a few hours later, and no one could have seen him do it. Except for Maggie.

How she was there, he didn't know. But that day, he had finally accepted that she had been watching him and knew the truth of who he was.

What he hadn't realized at the time was she had taken his notebook and tapes which contained all the evidence he would ever need against any of the men who might turn against him. Taken it and somehow hid it before he took them to the airport. She must have suspected what he was planning to do to her and didn't want the evidence to be lost. And even though he had torn the house apart looking for it, he couldn't find it.

After a year passed, and there was no sign of it, he relaxed. He decided that it must have been in the car after all and was now buried at the bottom of the lake.

All that meant was he had to collect the evidence again—a little more challenging the second time around. People were more paranoid. But he did it, and he kept the information safely hidden away. He had cameras in the room where it was so he knew if anyone came near it. No one had. He relaxed even more.

Until Alice grew up, and one day he felt her presence beside him on a business trip. He had stopped what he was doing, contacted the client, said he would try another time, the danger was too great, and then rushed home. Alice was outside working in the garden.

Seeing the car drive up, she ran to her dad and hugged him, just as she always did. And since he had never felt her presence again, he put it down to excess stress working for that particular client. Eventually, he completed the assignment, and everything returned to normal—for a time.

It was after Alice had moved away to go to school that he had started to worry again. Even though Alice sounded normal when she called him, she never had time to visit.

Leo hadn't been in his business all these years without knowing when something was wrong. So he had found Ace and hired him to seduce his daughter. Find out what she was doing. Did she know something? Was she hiding?

For over two years, Ace had said that all was fine. Until one day, Alice disappeared, and Leo knew she was running. He had screamed in rage when he realized he had been played all these years by a daughter who had pretended to love him. Instead, just like her mother, Alice had evidence of what he, and the men he worked for, were doing.

Leo didn't need proof of what he knew. It was the same feeling he had when he had found Maggie packing. Maybe Alice had known all along. Maybe her mother had told her. Or maybe Maggie had left a way for Alice to discover the notebook and tapes when she was old enough to know what they were. All those maybes made up one enormous danger. He had to find her and stop her before she told anyone else.

So when he had felt a presence again, at first, he thought it might be Alice. But it didn't feel like her. No, it was someone else. In the years following Maggie's death, Leo had read about people who could do things like remote viewing.

Most people thought it was all a farce, and he wanted to agree with them. But he had felt Maggie, and then Alice, and knew that somehow it must be true.

So Leo knew someone had been watching him.

Maybe it was a fluke, and they weren't looking for me, was what he told himself as he packed his bags. He had told his clients he was working on a private matter and would be back to work in a week.

Yes, Leo thought, *a very private matter.*

He knew that Maggie grew up in Pennsylvania. He'd head there and decide what to do next. Along the way, perhaps the person watching him would reveal himself, and he'd take care of that person along with Alice.

TWENTY SIX

G race watched Lex run back across the street and waved at
Valerie as she opened the door for her son. It wouldn't be
long before Valerie would ask her what Lex had told her, and
when that happened, she had to make a decision. Would she call
a meeting and talk about it? Would she just tell Valerie? Or would
she not tell anyone?

She hoped that Lex would do what she asked him to do so she
wouldn't have to decide. After all, his step-father, Craig, was part
of the original Stone Circle and had his own gifts, not just the
gift of healing as the town's doctor. Lex's brother Johnny had
been instrumental in helping many people with his gifts, which
included remote viewing. But Johnny also could see people who
lived in the in-between.

A few months ago, Johnny had helped Connie Matthews go
back in time after she died and change what she had done wrong
the first time around. It had been an interesting experience for all
of them and had a lovely outcome. However, only some people
remembered the changes made, and she was grateful that she was
one of them.

Maybe this experience would have a lovely outcome too. And
although Valerie didn't have any paranormal gifts, she was wise

and kind, which were the most important gifts of all in Grace's opinion. Yes, they were who Lex had to tell first. After that, they would need a meeting. It was possible the man Lex had seen was coming to Doveland because Thomas' granddaughter was on her way. Everyone needed to know to help protect her and Thomas.

Inside the house, Valerie hugged her son and then took him into the living room where Craig and Johnny were waiting. Lex took one look at them and realized that Grace was right. He needed to tell them. She hadn't been freaked out by what he had said. Why would his family? Especially this family.

It was Johnny who spoke first.

"Look, Lex. I know what it's like to discover something you can do that you didn't know you could. It was terrifying when it happened to me, especially since I didn't know what was happening.

"And even now, sometimes I don't know if I can handle it. But the one thing I have learned, and I know you already understand, is that you can't do this on your own. Tell us what's going on so we can help."

It wasn't the fact that Lex had remote viewed that got Valerie out of her seat to call Grace. It was that she was alarmed by what he told them. If they had listened to Lex when he had tried to tell them the first time, they would have prepared sooner.

"I already called Ava," Grace said before Valerie said anything. "Figured we needed to meet?"

Valerie glanced out the window to see Hank's truck pull up opposite the Diner.

"Could you tell Hank? He just went into the Diner with Thomas."

Lex whispered, "Tommy, he wants to be called Tommy by his friends."

"Tommy," Valerie corrected herself, remembering how Lex knew that. She saw Craig put his arm around both Lex and Johnny and pull them close, and she said thank you to whoever was responsible for bringing such a good man into her life.

Before Grace hung up, she said, "Valerie, let's remember what Sarah always told us. Good has more power than evil. We've proved that over and over, and we'll prove it again."

"Yes," Valerie answered before hanging up. "Yes, we will."

They might not have felt so confident if they knew who was coming their way.

· · · ● · ● · ● · ·

Thomas pulled into the Diner not long after Hank, so when Grace walked in, she had everyone there who she wanted to tell about the meeting.

That Grace was in the Diner at all stopped all the conversation. Pete was the first to snap himself out of it and rushed to the door to welcome her to his "humble abode," as he said.

Grace laughed and said she came for pancakes. She had no idea why she said that, but Grace realized that was exactly what she wanted. Thomas and Hank asked if they could join her, and the three of them took a booth at the back of the Diner. Pete went to work on the pancakes, and Barbara slid in the booth too.

It was early, so not that many people were there yet. A family headed for the lake, probably to fish, and a few members of Hank's construction crew getting some food before heading to Thomas' house.

"How's it going at your house, Tommy," Grace asked.

Thomas looked at Hank, his face filled with admiration.

"I can't believe how quickly this is happening. It's like an army of ants over there, all working together. I've never seen anything like it. I thought trades didn't work together that way. And all those young kids helping. It's a beautiful thing, Hank."

Hank couldn't help it. He beamed with pride. But it was Grace who told Thomas what he was seeing.

"Hank is mentoring many of the young people of Concourse and Doveland. He and his friend Melvin started a school where the trades are taught. To be on his crew, you have to agree to teach and work together as a community.

"The few people that couldn't work that way have gone to work for other construction crews in town. But he never has a lack of people who want to work with him. Yes, he pays well, but I think they like the atmosphere and the feelings they get from helping the young people."

Hank nodded. "I know I love it. Yes, it takes a little extra time to stop and show something. We teach them how to do these things at our headquarters on Melvin Byler's old farm. But doing it for real always has extra challenges. But they are all becoming quite skilled. My best worker right now is a young girl from Concourse."

Thomas shook his head. "All this was going on while I was holed up in my house, hoping to die. Doing nothing."

He swept his hand around to include the Diner and the town outside. "I missed all this. What a waste of time."

Grace reached across and patted his hand just as Pete brought over a stack of pancakes and four plates along with everything anyone could ever want to put on pancakes.

"Well, we are delighted to have you here now. Sometimes it takes a monumental event to wake us up to what we are missing in life. And that one for you is your granddaughter, Alice."

Although Thomas smiled and nodded before tucking into his pancakes, Pete, Barbara, and Hank caught the underlying meaning in Grace's words. Something else was going on, and they needed to talk about it.

TWENTY SEVEN

Duke sat back in the car and pulled the partition closed between him and his driver. He could see the driver. The driver couldn't see him. However, it wouldn't have mattered. His face was a mask—a mask that looked like an actual face. It was amazing what they could do now with technology, especially when you could hire the best. He had a variety of masks and wore them depending on who he was meeting. This was the face his driver had seen for years as he got in and out of the car.

It had been a long time since anyone had seen his actual face. Not that he bothered to see anyone in person most of the time. He could see them anytime he wanted to. The people who worked for him never could understand how he would know things, things that were impossible for him to know.

And yet he did. They all were terrified as they worked for him, which is how he wanted it. But they had all had a choice in the beginning. He had told them he would always be watching them. Of course, it wasn't him that watched most of them. One of his people did, but they were warned. Were they sure they wanted the job even under those conditions?

Very few walked away from the job. The lure of the money and the power Duke offered was too much for most people to turn down. He always tailored the offer to give them what they wanted most. Of course, he investigated them first, so it was easy to offer them what they most desired.

Some wanted power, some wanted money, some wanted prestige. Some wanted what passed for love. He gave them that. Whatever they asked for. In exchange, they sold their life to him. He needed physical bodies in the world to do the physical things that needed to be done.

Only a few people walked away. He admired them for it. And then Duke went back to see what he had done wrong, found where he had missed the mark in what he offered them. Then he called them back and offered them that. About half took him up on it, but Duke didn't hire them. He got rid of them. They could be bribed.

However, the ones that turned him down the second time walked away, free. He watched them through the years, though, wondering if it had been a ruse. But it gave him a strange sense of pleasure when they had turned him down the second time. They knew what was important to them. Not what he could offer. At least not at the price he demanded.

Those people lived what he considered insignificant lives. But he could tell they lived happy lives. Some even succeeded without him, which meant that eventually they became his enemies if they stood in the way of what he wanted.

But for the very few that never got in his way and were obviously content and happy, he found himself cheering them on. It gave him a perverse sense of pleasure to know that happiness existed somewhere. Not the kind he experienced, but the kind that he assumed meant something.

Alice had been one of those people. She had turned him down every time.

Duke shook his head at the memory. He had tried everything—except force. That was against his principles. Not because he didn't like force, but in the beginning, it turned people against him. After they were indebted to him, yes, he used force.

With Alice, nothing Duke tried worked. Alice said no. Kindly at first and then with more strength and then back to kindness and compassion mixed with a steely resolve.

Yes, he had admired her for that. And would have left her alone. Beautiful women were everywhere—beautiful, intelligent, and willing women. He could always get them to work for him. Besides, it wasn't her beauty or intelligence he wanted around him. It was because of who she was—part of a distant past.

So he watched her. And when he saw what she was planning, he had to stop her.

What he hadn't reckoned on were her abilities to block him. A little too late since he had already seen her plans, but not too late to keep him from knowing where she was going now.

That blast of mental energy he sent to her should have killed her, even though he hated the idea of doing it. Instead, she lost her memory. But obviously not enough to unconsciously know she was in danger and keep herself safe.

He had made too many mistakes around Alice and her family. He made the first one years before. But it was too late to fix that. Now he had to close out the past. Forever.

He knew where Alice was going. To her grandfather. Even without her memory, she was heading there like a homing pigeon. Not knowing why, but doing it anyway.

And he knew where Thomas Hendrick lived. It didn't surprise him that Thomas had moved there. It was his wife's hometown.

He should have taken care of Thomas Hendrick years ago. It was a hole in his life that made him vulnerable, and he hated being weak. He would bet his life that was where Alice was heading. And that was not an idle thing to say. It was his life on the line.

Doveland wasn't far from the airport. He would get there first and take care of that old man who took away what had been so precious to him. Then Alice, because of what she knew. And then all the other people that had made such a mess of this.

Duke pushed the intercom and screamed, "Go faster!" He watched as his car passed other cars and trucks. He wasn't worried about being noticed.

His driver knew that they would never be pulled over. And he would always do what Mr. Quinn told him to do. Part of him hoped they crashed. Yes, he would die. But so would that monster in his back seat, and his family would be free.

Duke knew that cloaking the car, and keeping it on the road, would drain most of his energy, so he made one last phone call.

"I'll be there soon. Have my plane ready," before laying his head back on the seat, closing his eyes, and concentrating on getting them to the airport safely.

It occurred to him that if he continued to live so far away from people, he needed a helicopter pad. This driving to places was too hard on him. Took too much time. He'd add that to the list of things to have one of his people attend to.

He loved having people at his beck and call. Power was all he ever wanted, and now that girl was trying to take it away. He couldn't let her.

TWENTY EIGHT

The three of them stayed the night at the motel, and in the morning, they turned in the rental car and they all piled into James' car. Not the one he had driven in. A new one. Evie shook her head at the memory, both amused and amazed that someone could simply trade one car for another without worrying about the price. And he paid cash. And he registered it in a different name. No one asked questions. Apparently, with cash, it didn't matter that he never showed them identification.

Afterward, sitting in the local restaurant eating breakfast before getting on the road, she and Owen asked the obvious questions. Where did he get all that money? And how did he know how to do these things? And why?

"The why part is obvious, young lady." James had said. "You told me you were hiding and running away. As far as the how to do it part? I watch a lot of TV shows."

When both Evie and Owen looked at him with squinted eyes, he added, "Everyone knows to use cash when they are running, don't they? After all, look at you, Evie. You pay in cash. That's not your actual hair color, and traveling with your new brother is an excellent cover, right?"

Evie took a sip of her coffee.

"But eventually, they will discover that you sold your old car and track that you bought a new one."

"You're right. It will only slow them down. But then I bought that car in another name too, so it will take a few days before they figure it out. That is assuming someone is looking. Which I doubt. I'm just a pizza shop owner."

"But the money?" Owen asked. He had less than twenty dollars in his pocket. Money wasn't driving his decisions, but to have that much money seemed impossible.

"Oh, that reminds me," James said, reaching into his pocket. "I forgot to give you your back pay before you left."

"Back pay?"

"Sure. I was putting it aside until you decided what you wanted to do, and now that you know that being this young lady's brother is what you want to do, I can turn it over to you. It was burning a hole in my pocket, anyway."

Owen took a quick look at the money clip that James handed him and tried to hand it back.

"Owen, you earned it. You will earn it. You have something special going for you, and I am grateful to be part of it and help you along. I have more money than I could ever spend. After the two of you left, I realized that what I wanted to do was to be of service. That means I can spread the wealth. Let me."

When Owen nodded, trying not to cry, James turned his attention to Evie.

"Now, young lady. We have been saying 'they,' but do you have any idea who 'they' are?"

Evie shook her head, no.

"I have pictures that flash in my head now, so I hope that my memories are returning. All I know is that I can never get rid of the fear that someone is after me, and someone can see me wherever I am.

"And although I appreciate both of you more than I can say, it worries me that I am bringing you into something that could be dangerous to anyone who knows me, let alone helps me."

Owen had laughed at that.

"Are you kidding? This is the most exciting thing to ever happen to me. I promise you I am sufficiently afraid too, but this gives me a chance to see what I can do. It's got to be more than working in a pizza shop. Sorry, Mr. Cahill," he added, looking down.

James laughed too. "Well, that says it all for me too. I too want to find out what I am capable of. Not just being the owner of a pizza shop."

Evie looked at the two men who had decided to help her. One, a young boy just starting out in life, his brown hair falling into his eyes, wearing clothes that were just a little too small for him. She knew his parents had decided he didn't belong to them because he was different, and that made him wrong.

And then there was James, who had lived a successful business life, but to hear him tell it he had failed at his personal life. He and Owen looked vaguely alike, although James was shorter than Owen. Both of them had brown eyes, although James' hair sat way back on his head and was a dull gray. She supposed that they could pass for father and son if needed. She was the one that didn't fit in, but that happened in families, didn't it? They could just say that she looked like her dead mother.

Evie realized that helping her helped them find a relationship that James had lost, and Owen never had. It hadn't eased her mind much, but it helped her make a decision, one that she hoped she would not live to regret. Actually, she hoped they all lived to find out what was really going on.

So she had nodded at the two of them and reached out and held both their hands. "Okay, my little brother and my dad. Let's hit the road."

116

Evie didn't have a license, but they decided to chance it. They would all keep to the speed limit, and the three of them would trade off driving. That way, James thought, they could make it to Pennsylvania within the next day or two.

Evie had hesitated at first. It was a risk if they were stopped, but the pressure she felt was mounting. She was not only afraid for herself, and now Owen and James, but there was a little kernel of terror growing inside her for whoever was at that address.

Everything pointed to getting there as quickly as possible. So Evie had gulped, nodded, and took the wheel first. They traded off every few hours, usually at a rest stop, sometimes at a drive-through restaurant.

The closer they got to Pennsylvania, the more terrified Evie became. Yes, whatever was chasing her knew where she was going. And as flashes of memory returned, Evie knew it was more than one person coming to stop her. From doing what, she still didn't know. But once they got to Doveland, she hoped they would find out in time.

TWENTY NINE

This time they met in Grace's apartment above her coffee shop. Grace had brought up pastries and drinks. Unlike their dinner parties, it was a somber group of people who gathered together. They needed answers.

"What do you know that you haven't told us, Tommy?" Grace asked after everyone was seated.

Alex Bender was running the Diner, so Pete and Barbara could be at the meeting. They were sitting on one of the two facing couches. Hank sat beside them.

Ava had dropped Ben off at preschool, and she and Evan sat together on the opposite couch.

After getting Lex to tell them all that he experienced, Craig had taken him to school before heading to work as the town's doctor, so only Valerie and Johnny had come to the meeting. Valerie sat beside Ava, and Johnny perched on the arm of the couch.

Sitting in opposite chairs, Grace faced Thomas across the large coffee table that sat between them all.

They were in her living room, designed for meetings like this. Light filled the room, but the mood was dark.

Thomas fidgeted in his chair, ran his hands through his hair, and said, "I have nothing else to tell you. Or, at least I don't know what you mean by the question."

Looking around the room, he added, "You all seem so upset. But by what?"

"He doesn't know."

Everyone turned to look at Johnny, who had stood and walked to one of the windows that looked out over the town's park. The view from Grace's window differed slightly from the one from their house, and that seemed an excellent analogy to him. Everyone has a different view of the world around them.

Johnny also knew that most people didn't see all that was going on around them. For example, everyone could see Bryan and Rachel sitting on one of the park's benches holding hands. High school friends, they had finally married a few months before, and he knew they were supremely happy.

But that's not all that was going on. Johnny could also see that they were talking to someone who lived in the in-between. Not a ghost. Not a spirit. Someone who had died but hadn't moved on for whatever reason. It was Bryan's "job" to help them, and Rachel helped Bryan.

Yes, he saw things others didn't see. It didn't make him better or worse. But they couldn't assume that everyone knew there was more than what could be detected by the five very limited senses. And even if they knew, it didn't mean they could experience it.

Turning back from the window, Johnny said, "Tommy doesn't know what you are asking him. And he doesn't know why you are upset. We have to tell him more so he knows what and why you are asking."

Grace reached up and grabbed Johnny's hand and smiled at him. "Thank you for reminding us."

Thomas looked around the room. He had thought these people were the most kind and generous people he had ever met. They had turned his life around by helping him without hesitation. Now it occurred to him they were even more than that.

"What are you people?" Thomas asked.

It was Valerie who answered him.

"Regular people. Except some of us have what other people call magical or paranormal gifts."

Thomas looked less astonished than they thought he would. First, he looked closely at each one of them and then threw back his head and laughed.

"Who knew this would all come back to me," he said once he stopped laughing.

"And I know it's not a laughing matter, but you wouldn't believe how often I tried to get people to believe me. And how close I was to proving something so important. And then to get ostracized and then fired and then given a mental health warning. And now, to find myself in the middle of an average group of people, in the town where my wife grew up, who claim to be doing 'magical' things. Well, it's just too funny. I was missing what was around me the whole time I was moping in my house.

"But at least I think I understand the question now. You want to know what I was researching and what I found."

Everyone stared at Thomas, dumbfounded.

"Well, obviously, we missed it too," Grace said. "I know we have many questions, but perhaps you might want to ask yours first."

"The most important question is, does this all have something to do with my granddaughter?"

"We think it does," Valerie answered.

Thomas sighed deeply. "Now, I am afraid. And that's what you are too, isn't it? Afraid."

"Not afraid, Tommy," Valerie said, "On alert."

"Perhaps I would be less afraid if you told me what you mean by paranormal powers. Who does what here?"

"Well, that could take a long time," Grace said. "Lots of stories to tell, which we will tell you when there is time. We all are different. Some of us have nothing 'magical.' And those that do, we call them gifts.

"We try not to use the word paranormal. What's normal anyway? Some of the gifts have been revealed to us as we work together, and some of us knew about them before we met. But what you need to know is that we don't think we are special. We just want to use what we can to help. And you called this meeting because Valerie's son Lex 'saw' someone coming to Doveland that has evil intentions."

"More than one person," Johnny added.

"Saw?"

"We call it remote viewing. Do you know it?"

"Not only do I know it, but I was also studying the phenomena and researching it. Most people think it doesn't exist. I did."

"What else were you studying?" Grace asked.

"I am almost afraid to say. Don't laugh, please. Time travel. Dimension travel."

It was Hank who started laughing this time.

"Dang, wasn't expecting that." Seeing Thomas' face, Hank said, "Nope. Not laughing at you. Laughing at us for missing what is going on."

"You believe in it?"

Grace sighed. "Believe in it. Lived it."

121

THIRTY

Later that day, Thomas sat with Hank and Evan in the kitchen while Ava put the Thai food that they had ordered onto plates for each of them.

"I probably shouldn't be hungry," Thomas said. "But I am."

"Me, too," Ava added, as she put the plates on the table. "That's a good thing. All of it, really. To be hungry and then have something so delicious to eat. Not only that, I didn't have to cook it!"

The four of them picked up their water glasses and clinked them together.

Once everyone had eaten enough to talk again, Thomas asked the obvious question.

"What happens now?"

"I told the police chief, Daniel Winters, that your granddaughter is coming to visit you, and that there is a possibility that some 'bad-men' were coming after her. He will watch for strangers, and he has increased the security around your house and here."

"He believed you?"

Ava smiled at Thomas.

"Dan has seen some strange things happening in town. He doesn't understand it, but he accepts that when we tell him something, we probably know what we are talking about."

"And," Evan added, "this property is very secure."

"Past events?" Thomas asked.

All three nodded.

"Not sure how the fact that I was studying the possibilities of portals into other dimensions would put my granddaughter at risk. I was easy enough to stop, wasn't I? I just gave up."

"I think the question is, who was upset enough with what you were studying to stop you in the first place? And why? There are many scientists who are turning their attention to these studies. Perhaps it's not mainstream, but it is definitely not unknown."

"Which makes me wonder if it's not about that exactly. Besides, why would Alice be in danger just because you studied something? Do they not want Alice to find you because that brings you back to life, so to speak? Or is it something entirely different? Maybe something to do with your missing daughter? How long has it been since you have seen her?"

Thomas pushed back from the table and began walking around the kitchen.

"She ran away over twenty years ago. Never got in touch with me again. For all I know, she died. But she could still be alive, couldn't she? Maybe Maggie is coming with Alice?"

For a moment, Thomas' face lit up.

"Except, why was it Alice who wrote if that were true?"

Thomas sat down again, looking ten years older.

"I have to accept that Maggie probably died, don't I?"

No one tried to tell him differently. There was no point in giving him false hope. If Maggie were still alive, then they would celebrate with him. But right now, they needed to make sure he and his granddaughter remained safe until they figured out who was after them and why. And stopped them.

All of which was difficult when they knew nothing about where Alice was, or who was after her, or why, or when any of them would arrive. That's why both Lex and Johnny were going to try to remote view them and see if they could find out more.

When Ava's phone beeped she looked at her text, hoping that Valerie had good news.

Her face fell as she read, "Whoever Lex saw before must know what happened and is now blocking them."

After dinner, Hank walked Thomas to the bunkhouse, made sure everything was secure, and then headed to Thomas' home, where he would sleep from now on. Yes, they had guards at his house, but Hank knew what it felt like to find family and then be afraid to lose it.

He had found Ava, his sister's daughter, and that had opened a floodgate of friends he now called family. He would do anything to keep them safe. And he wanted Thomas to have the same experience. He would keep Thomas and his little family safe. He would do whatever it took.

Hank knew he had one thing helping him that most people didn't have. He knew how evil men thought. He had worked for one most of his life until he found Ava. He had been one. Although he had been forgiven by those he had hurt, and he had made an uneasy peace with his past, deep down, he still worried that he would always be a bad man.

The only thing that calmed his fear was knowing that he was never an evil man. Yes, he had done bad things. But bad and evil were two different things. He was not evil. He had never based his life on greed and power, never wanted to control others through fear. At his worst, he had still cared. He knew there were men and women who had lost that ability, if they ever had it. Yes, he knew they existed, and that gave him an edge.

It was that kind of person Hank thought was coming to Doveland. Not because he had any magical or paranormal powers at all. What Hank had was what people called spidey senses. Everyone had them. Not everyone listened to them.

Hank did. He always had. His were honed. And they were tingling the same way they used to when his past boss, Grant Hinkley, had come after him and his family.

Grant was now dead. But there were always people who wanted to stop people who stood up for good, stop the people who couldn't be confused by misleading words and actions. Evil people wanted to get rid of the people who had good intentions and acted on them.

And Doveland was full of people with good intentions, and they acted on them. And now it was also the home of people who could do things like remote view, read minds, and see what others couldn't see. And that made Doveland a magnet for those that hated anything that had the power to see what wasn't good and stop it. Those dangerous people hated people who combined kindness and generosity with insight and courage.

It wasn't strange that Alice was coming to Doveland for help. But who was following her, and why? That's what they didn't know yet. However, Hank was reasonably sure that they would find out soon. That's why he hid his truck and snuck into Thomas' house. Even the guards didn't see him. Which meant that if he could sneak past them, so could someone else.

All the more reason to be here, Hank told himself, while he stationed himself where he could see everything. The roof. His phone and night vision binoculars beside him, he waited.

He would wait every night until he saw them. That's what he was good at. Waiting and watching and protecting. That was his gift.

THIRTY ONE

While Hank waited, Thomas did too. In his own way. He waited for something to tell him why Alice would be in danger. Was it from his work? Or was it from something Maggie did? Or something that Alice did? Or maybe something they both knew? But what would that be?

Thomas lay on his back on the bed, fully dressed. Lay his head on his hands and stared at the ceiling. Looking for answers. It was how he used to figure out things for work. He looked for patterns. Tried to imagine connections. Followed niggling ideas as they led him to another one. He had loved that work.

It amazed him that he had let them take it away from him. He should have seen the pattern of what they were doing. Discrediting him. Spreading rumors about his mental state. He had ignored it all, stopped paying attention to the whispers that would stop when he walked into a room. He had been a fool.

After meeting this group of people, he realized that he had been a fool for a long time. Instead of withdrawing from friends and only concentrating on his work, he should have reached out, let people into his life. He wouldn't make that mistake again.

Thomas laughed to himself. As if this group would let him.

Staring at the ceiling, Thomas eventually fell asleep. But even in sleep he was puzzling out the questions. Looking for patterns.

• • • ● • ● • • •

Not far away, the family group that now called themselves Evie, Owen, and James Lynn, paused one last time.

Earlier that day, they had turned off the I80 and were heading south towards Doveland when they saw a sign for an outlet mall. Evie squealed, shocking even herself.

Was she a squealer? How embarrassing, she had thought.

But neither James nor Owen seemed to mind. In fact, they looked at each other and smiled, and then Owen, who had been driving, took the exit to the outlet.

"This is a good idea," James said once they parked. "Food, and then some therapy shopping?"

"Therapy shopping?" Evie said. "You know about therapy shopping?"

"I may be old, but I'm not stupid," James replied, smiling at her. "My wife used to talk about it. I tried it a few times myself. Besides, we are all in need of new clothes. Let's get clothes. We'll rent a few rooms and get some sleep and a shower before heading into Doveland. Whatever we find there, we probably want to look our best, right?"

Evie leaned forward and gave James a hug, which included his seat.

"In case something happens to me, I want you to know that I think these may have been the happiest days of my life. Traveling with the two of you."

Owen turned in his seat to see her and James.

"Me too. It seems strange given that we are hiding from who knows what and running to who knows who, but this has been wonderful."

"Hey, kids," James said, infusing the most hope he could muster into his voice, "It's not over yet. Maybe it will never be over. And no matter what happens, you two should know that you have made me a happy man too. "Maybe it only gets better from here!"

Evie smiled, and the three of them high-fived, but none of them really believed that. They knew it would get worse first. But there was the possibility that after whatever was going on was over, they could have more adventures together.

Yes, Evie thought to herself. It was possible. But during the past few days, more images were coming to her, and none of them made her feel safer. Only one made her happy. A woman was leaning over her and telling her how much she loved her.

Who was that woman? And did it have something to do with what was happening?

Evie believed that her memory was returning, and for that she was grateful. But would it return in time, and was the person they were heading towards someone that would give her the answers?

But when Owen opened the back door and extended his hand to help her out of the car, saying, "Let's go, sis," she couldn't help smiling. Right here and right now, she would choose to enjoy herself and her new family.

Later, in the motel room, she looked in the mirror and almost recognized herself. With the help of a saleswoman, she had found hair dye to match her roots. Now she could see someone that felt familiar. Red hair, strange blue eyes. Just like the woman who had leaned over her in her memory.

Evie stared at the mirror, willing herself to remember that woman. Was she alive? Did she love her? When a strange warm feeling came over her, Evie reasoned it was the warmth in the bathroom from the long shower she had taken that had caused that sensation.

But what if it's more than that, she wondered.

They had rented three connecting rooms. Splurging, James had said. For the bathrooms. But Evie had asked Owen if she could sleep in the other bed in his room, and he agreed, trying not to show how happy he was that Evie felt safe with him.

Owen heard the faint knock on his door and yelled, "come in." He yelled again when he saw Evie, which brought James running through the other connecting door.

He started to say, "Is everything all right?" But instead stood there with his mouth open, looking just like Owen, until one of them said, "Wow!"

Evie had stopped in the doorway, hands over her mouth, tears running down her face at their reaction.

"Wow, good?" she whispered.

"Wow, amazing," Owen said and rushed over to hug her.

"Group hug," he said, and pulled James in.

Not one of them said out loud what they were thinking. If only this could last and worried that it couldn't.

THIRTY TWO

Duke Quinn hated hotels attached to airports, but the Marriott at the Pittsburgh airport was much too convenient to ignore, and it wasn't as bad as some of them.

On the plane, he had been one person. At the hotel, he was another. Different name. Different face. Always for the cameras and for the people who were always watching for him. He knew they were too incompetent to find him. Despite that, one could never be too careful. And he always cloaked himself so that those amateur—compared to him—remote viewers could never find him. Although that kid did, but that was a fluke. Duke had been searching for Alice and must have let his guard down for a second.

That's what Duke told himself, and he was tempted to ignore that it had happened. It was probably an accident. The kid was obviously new at the process and had most likely tuned into his frequency by mistake. However, when he traced back to where the kid's signal had come from, and it turned out to be a small town in Pennsylvania, and one he knew well, he couldn't discount it.

He knew that patterns existed, connections ran the world, and he had made his fortune by following those patterns and connections. And then by controlling where they took him.

Duke could have gone straight to Doveland. It wasn't that far from the airport. But he had work to do first. And he was tired. He was tired of the work. He was tired of dealing with lowly beings so far removed from who he had made himself into.

As a child, he had been the punching bag both verbally and physically for what felt like every bully in town. And then one day he discovered his gift, and after that everything changed. It was the day he stopped one of the school bullies who was in mid-punch by yelling "stop!" It shocked not only him but everyone watching.

He thought it was a fluke. They left him alone anyway. Testing what he had learned, Duke went home and stopped his father from picking up the next bottle of beer by telling him to stop.

His father had turned to look at him and then stumbled to bed. Duke had thrown every bottle of liquor out that night and then sat at the table waiting for morning to come.

When his father staggered out of the bedroom and opened the refrigerator to grab his first bottle of beer for the day and saw that they were missing, he headed for Duke, ready to do what he always did. Throw him around. This time it wouldn't just be a toss across the room. This time his father's fury was like a flaming dagger heading right towards him.

Duke stood, all four feet eleven inches of him, at ten years old, and said, "stop." Arms across his chest, legs planted as wide as he could, he glared. His father stopped, but the fury was still there.

It was at that moment that Duke made a decision that changed their lives. He knew that he could twist the fury his father felt so it was no longer directed at Duke, but back at his father.

Duke had witnessed the destructive nature of hatred and rage unleashed his whole life. Had watched his father's friends as they fought for no reason. Had seen the fury in the eyes of the boys that beat him for fun.

Twisting his fury against him, he could get rid of his father forever. But in that split second, Duke realized it would be better to use his father instead. After all, he was still a boy. He had no money. Too young to work. They would take him away to live with someone else.

No, he thought, *it would be better to stay with this man.*

It wasn't out of kindness that Duke said, "Stop it. You don't need to feel that anymore."

Duke's words took a few moments to sink into his father's being. As he got older, Duke became a master of words spoken and unspoken. He became eloquent in his clarity and simplicity.

But that day, it worked anyway. Maybe because it was his father. Perhaps it was pure luck. Duke chuckled at the memory. The feeling of power he had that day had invaded every pore of his being. His father had stopped, looked at Duke as if he didn't know who he was, and went back to bed.

He stayed there for two days. Duke considered that a victory. It meant he was free to do whatever he wanted to do. At first, he spent money he found in his father's wallet on things he wanted. Starting with good food. He went to school and glared at the boys, who only once more attempted to bully him. He used his newfound power, and they obeyed. "Never hurt me again." They didn't. Well, they couldn't.

After that, he ruled them. He enjoyed making them do things they wanted to do but were afraid to. He took away their mental constraints and let them run wild. And run wild, they did. By the time they reached high school, they had all been arrested, and since he last checked, all but one had died violently. Not because of him. He didn't need to waste any energy on them after the first few months of getting them in trouble.

By that time, they were missing the piece of themselves that told them what they were doing was wrong. But they were also missing the intelligence to direct wrath in ways that would help them. So they didn't survive.

Duke didn't care about those boys, but he learned from them. That's what unintelligent beings did to themselves. He knew then that he would never be like them in that way. With his gift of mental manipulation, he could control, but intelligently. Always for himself. He would let others destroy themselves with his suggestions. He could control anyone and anything.

Or so he thought. Then he had learned that he couldn't control some people. And that had worried him enough that he decided to find out what they had that others didn't. All they seemed to have that was different was a strong moral code and an intention only to do good.

It had been such a simple answer that he discounted it for years. Then he tried to destroy that in them. The same way he hired people. Bit by bit. Yes, some of them caved, but most of them did not.

They had what he didn't have. He knew he had been missing it from the beginning. It was why those bullies had picked on him. They knew that they had to destroy him before he destroyed them.

They had not attacked him because he was weak, but because despite their base stupidity, they had recognized someone just like them, but worse. Someone who could make others do what he wanted them to and didn't care who or how he hurt anyone.

Yes, the day he saved his father, he had made a wise decision. After two days in bed, his father had gotten up and gone to work. From that day until he died, he made sure that his boy had everything he needed.

The day Duke turned eighteen, he suggested to his father that he kill himself. His father obliged. Duke buried him according to his wishes, sold the house, and moved away.

And now, here he was. Home again. Back where it all began. It was time to put an end to it for good.

Of course, he hadn't been Duke Quinn then. He had been someone else.

THIRTY THREE

Ace wondered if he was the stupidest man on the planet. What did he think? That he would drive to Pennsylvania, cross the state line, and immediately know where Alice had gone?

He pulled off the road in someplace called Moon Township, near the Pittsburgh airport, and wondered if he had gone to the moon because it was just as likely that he would find Alice in Pennsylvania as it was he would on the moon.

Since pulling out of the McDonald's a few days before and almost hitting that guy's car, Ace had moved between terror and a sense of purpose. What that purpose was, he wasn't sure. He just felt that perhaps he had one.

Maybe it was as simple as finding Alice and protecting her from Leo. Once he heard himself think that he would protect Alice, he started worrying about his state of mind. How had he gone from being the person who spied on her for her father to one who wanted to protect her?

When did that happen? It was only after she went missing that he felt the part of his heart that had opened enough to let her in. He remembered nights with her as she snuggled up against him and fell asleep with her head on his shoulder.

It was confusing. If Alice knew her father was after her all along, and if she figured out he was working for her father, why was she so loving and kind to him? Because she was.

Yes, she was distant, and now he knew that she had also been hiding what she was doing from him, but could all of that kindness and sweetness they sometimes shared have been fake?

Somewhere in Indiana, Ace had faced the fact that he had fallen for Alice without meaning to and hadn't even noticed. Until now. Now that he was chasing her.

He knew Leo would be furious, and he would make him pay for protecting Alice, but what could he do? What did Alice do that was so bad that her own father hired him to keep tabs on her? At the time, it wasn't to hurt her, only to report back what she was doing and look for a notebook and some tapes.

"Well, I don't know if it is still a notebook and tapes," Leo had said. "She could have copied them. Maybe a thumb-drive?"

"What's on the tapes? What does the notebook look like?" Ace had asked.

"Don't be stupid," Leo had shouted back. "You'll know it when you see it. Names, dates, notes. Don't read it, just get it back to me."

Even then, Ace knew that if he found it, he was a dead man because if it was something that Leo would hunt down his daughter for, he would definitely get rid of a worthless man like himself.

Yes, he knew what he was. He had been told often enough. And yet, he could have sworn that the beautiful Alice had fallen for him. Maybe just a little.

It was that hope and the hope that he could be more than just the man who spied on her that drove him on. With every mile he tried to remember where Alice had told him her mother had come from.

He knew that she had told him once. Why had she told him? Did she tell him before she realized who he was and what he was doing?

Or did she want him to know? That was what he was hoping—that she had told him as an insurance policy, hoping he would choose to protect her if he could.

It was a stupid thought, Ace knew. If that were true, why did she run away from him? What had happened?

Ace knew Leo wouldn't have hired just him to watch his daughter. There had to be others, but none of them would have known about each other. That meant every stranger was dangerous. Leo used that tactic to control people.

But Ace told himself Leo didn't know where he was, so for the moment driving down route 376, he was safe. He hoped.

Still, he was exhausted and clueless about where he was going, which is how he ended up in Moon Township sleeping in a Super 8, waiting for a bolt of inspiration to strike so he would know where he was going.

In the morning, after eating the continental breakfast, he went outside and leaned against the building, looking at the trees and the almost empty parking lot, and he remembered.

It wasn't a bolt of lightning, after all. It was a pair of doves walking across the parking lot towards the trees. He had watched them, remembering how his mother told him doves mated for life.

Why did birds have all the luck, he had thought, and then he remembered.

Alice had told him her mother came from a town called Doveland.

Slapping his forehead, he had whispered thank you to the doves, thinking that maybe he wasn't so evil that he couldn't thank some birds, and headed into the motel to pack and get a new map.

• • • • ● • ● • • •

Leo had been thinking the same thing. How did he think he was going to find Alice just by driving to Pennsylvania? Was there going to be a blinking sign along the highway that said, "Just follow the signs to your daughter."

And yet, in a way, that is almost what happened. After crossing over the Ohio-Pennsylvania line, he had taken Route 376 heading to Pittsburgh. He had been on the I80 for so long he thought he would never get off it, so driving down the broad, practically empty, tree-lined highway was a relief.

But he was tired, and he had no idea where to go next, so he took the first off-ramp that promised food and a place to stay. Besides, he had to make sure none of his clients were freaking out because he took a few days off.

Leo had always prided himself on knowing exactly what to do and when. His clients had expected that of him, and yet for the last few days, he had driven like a madman, not knowing exactly where he was going and not checking in. It was bad for business no matter how he looked at it, all because of Alice.

Thinking he could get some sleep while he figured out where he was going, Leo had pulled into the parking lot of the Super 8 just in time to see Ace slap his forehead and head into the motel.

Patterns. Leo had always believed in the theory that people circled each other and that some people repeated lifetimes together.

He had used that theory to do his job. Now it was showing him the way. All he had to do was wait for Ace to come out of the motel and follow him, because he was sure that Ace knew where Alice had gone.

His clients would have to wait. This was more important. Because if they knew what Alice's mother had taken, and now Alice had, they would want this to be the thing he was doing.

But they could never know. And they wouldn't, because he would get to Alice first and eliminate the threat.

THIRTY FOUR

Ava grabbed her purse and headed to the car with Ben in tow. Ben was excited. He loved school, for which Ava was grateful. And Evan was happy in his office, so she was free to do whatever she wanted to that morning.

Evan had turned one bedroom into an office where he worked most of the day. He could do that while watching over the few people that stayed at their private bed and breakfast.

From there he also ran a small business with his friend Tom, selling Tom's art online.

In the beginning, Tom's art had been just a hobby. But after he was asked to sketch the man who had died on the park bench a few years before, his wife Mandy had suggested turning it into a business.

The man on the bench had been Joshua Lane. He had been searching for a lost sister. His grandson, Josh Baines, had recognized his grandfather from the picture Tom drew. The unraveling of where she had gone had brought more than one family together. It had also reunited Josh and Emily, who had met years before but had fallen out of touch.

Patterns. The twists and turns of life, Ava thought. *The gathering of people who have known each other through lifetimes.*

It was the idea of karass that Kurt Vonnegut wrote about in his novel Cat's Cradle. It was the thread that ran through everything she and her friends believed. They had a purpose together. Sometimes it was something as simple as providing support when needed.

Other times it was to help someone find the one they loved. Like Emily and Josh. And now Thomas and his granddaughter, Alice.

It was work that pleased her, and she was grateful for it, but right at that moment, she was thankful that Emily had built Emily's Hill, the retreat and art center north of town. It was where her daughter, Hannah, had taken dance lessons. And it was now where she took yoga at least twice a week.

When the weather was nice, like today—a beautiful warm fall day—they held the class outside on the large deck that jutted out from the hill, making it a favorite with everyone.

Emily's Hill had slowly developed, with Hank's help, and now housed not only movement classes of all kinds but also writing, music, and art classes. Evan came out to the hill once a week to take art classes, and in the summer, when Emily brought in guest artists, he attended those master workshops, hoping to help Tom more. But Emily suspected it was also because he too had fallen in love with making art.

Today, the parking lot was full, everyone wanting to get in as many outdoor classes as possible before the weather got too cold, and they moved the classes into the "barn." Not that it wasn't beautiful too, but outside with the birds singing, the different colored leaves waving in the wind, and the clouds sliding across a brilliant blue sky, to Ava, it was like entering God's cathedral.

She rolled out her mat and folded into a child's pose to wait for the class to begin. She loved that everyone respected the quiet before the class. Emily never played music when they had class outside. Nature provided all they wanted to hear.

By the time class was over, the worry over Thomas and his granddaughter had faded into the background enough to think clearly, or more accurately, feel clearly.

Although before coming to Doveland, Ava had no unique gifts, like many of the people in their karass, she had developed a few over the last few years. Well, not developed them. Let them come forward.

She couldn't remote view or travel to other dimensions, but she had helped Johnny, Bryan, and Rachel a few months before with a woman who was given a second chance, to go back in time and make things right after the woman died.

Ava knew about second chances. She had experienced them for herself and the ones she loved, and something about what was going on with Thomas had to do with second chances. Certainly, Thomas was being given a second chance, but it wasn't just him. Others, too.

And, although she couldn't see these people, she felt them. They were coming closer, but not all of them were coming for another chance. At least one of them was coming to stop them.

Ava bowed to Emily, smiled at her friends, blew a kiss to Josh, who watched from his writing studio where he was finishing another one of his popular books, and headed to town.

She called Grace as she drove, grateful that the phone connected through the car so she could concentrate on driving. She told Grace she was worried and needed to find Thomas.

That was all she had to say. Grace would take it from there. Ava didn't rush. She let herself flow along, trying to keep the sense of "all is right with the world" with her.

And she knew that no matter who or what wanted to disturb and harm the rightness of the world, they would never succeed in the long run. It was the short run that concerned her at the moment. She knew that just thinking good thoughts was not enough. Doing good required action.

By the time she parked her car across from the Diner, she could see Thomas and Hank in the window. She waved at Grace watching from Your Second Home and crossed the street, wondering exactly what she would say to Thomas.

Thomas, watching Ava cross the street, was wondering the same thing. What exactly did he know? Just a few days before, he had woken up from what he now realized had been a foolish and selfish decision to wait out the days until he died.

It had not occurred to him that he could and should be useful in the world. How could he have forgotten? The desire to know what else existed and to find underlying meaning had driven him his entire life, and he had been willing to walk away from it all.

But these people have given me a second chance, Thomas thought, *and I will do whatever is necessary to repay them for that.*

Both Hank and Thomas stood when the bell over the door tinkled and then gestured to the chair they had waiting for her.

"I ordered your favorite portobello burger, plus fries and coleslaw," Hank said.

"An Emily burger is coming up," Alex called from behind the counter.

Ava smiled. Not everyone had friends who had burgers named after them, or friends who knew her favorite lunch. She and Hank had managed their second chances together. Now they were part of Thomas' second chance. Like the portobello burger, it was a good thing.

THIRTY FIVE

J ames drove the last leg of their trip. Evie sat in the front seat looking at a map, guiding James towards their destination. There were a few tricky turns around Pittsburgh, but after they were outside the city and heading towards Doveland, Evie put the map down, laid her head against the seat, and closed her eyes.

"I'm so afraid," she finally said.

"More than you have been?" James asked, glancing quickly at Evie in time to see her brush away a tear.

"Yes. Which seems crazy. It feels as if I have been afraid all of my life. And what makes it worse is I don't remember why. Who am I?

"I try to tell myself it doesn't matter. After all, I have a new name, a new father and brother who left their own lives to help me with mine. I doubt many people experience that kind of family, real or chosen.

"Maybe we should forget this address and keep driving. We could go to someplace and start a new life."

Neither James nor Owen said anything. They waited, giving her time.

Finally, Owen spoke up.

"If that's what you want, Evie, I'll do it."

James nodded his agreement.

"But won't you still be afraid? Do you want to feel that way forever? Let's face what this is. Let's get some answers. Whoever is at that address must have some answers for you, don't you think?"

"But what if it's answers that I don't want to hear? What if it makes it worse?"

A long silence followed. Evie finally sighed and turned to James and Owen and said, "I know. The real question is, what if it makes it better."

James took one hand off the steering wheel and patted Evie's hand.

"That's my girl," he said. "Brave, courageous, and can we say again, beautiful!"

Evie laughed.

"You may. And now that all of us are all gussied up with our new clothes, let's go meet whoever lives at this address."

James and Owen smiled at her, and although they both were putting on their brave faces, she could feel their fear too. But they were right. They couldn't hide from it. They had to find out.

Glancing out the window, Evie admired what she saw—rolling hills, beautiful trees—but none of it looked familiar. She doubted she had ever been here before. She thought if she saw something familiar, it would help her memory. But nothing sparked anything.

As they got closer to Doveland, she had to keep glancing at the map to direct James. Heading east, they passed very few homes. She noticed a few mailboxes that told her that somewhere there were houses set far from the road.

A little tweak of joy surprised her when she realized a bike trail and a walking path ran parallel to the road. It was far off the road, to keep people safe. She would catch glimpses of it through the bushes and trees.

She had noticed it when they went through Concourse, but it amazed her it was still going. A trail connecting towns? People riding bikes and walking safely?

She loved it, and something about it reminded her of home. And herself. Perhaps she would walk that trail. She knew she loved to walk. That was something useful to know. It was a beginning.

At the end of the road they were traveling, they came to a stop sign. It was obviously the center of Doveland with a small park in the middle of the traffic circle. Around the circle, Evie glimpsed a few stores and a sign that said Town Hall.

She decided that the words traffic circle didn't fit because there wasn't any traffic. Most people were walking using the sidewalks. Or were in the tiny park. Just looking at it made her feel happy.

Evie asked if they could stop. The call to sit in the park was so strong she had to keep herself from opening the car door and dashing across the street to one of the benches.

James said, "Of course," turned right on the circle and pulled into a small grocery store's parking lot, thinking they could stock up on some food while they were there, and gas up at the tiny gas station that sat beside the store.

But he had no time to say anything before Evie had thrown open the door, crossed the street, and settled herself on a bench facing the Diner and what she now saw was a coffee shop named Your Second Home.

She decided that was where she wanted to go. But first, she needed to feel the sun on her face and smell the warm autumn air. A few moments later, James and Owen joined her, and they sat quietly together.

"I'm not afraid at this moment," Evie said, reaching for both their hands. "It's a wonderful feeling."

All three tipped their heads back, and let the sun play on their faces, and sighed together.

• • • ● • ● • • •

In the Diner, Thomas had just finished explaining to Ava and Hank that he had no answers about why Ava felt both fear and excitement. He felt both too. But he was feeling that way because he had never met his granddaughter. What would she be like? Would she like him? Was Alice coming to town the reason there was also the dark energy Ava and others had felt?

Hank had just paid for the food when Thomas glanced out the window at the park and fell back into his seat, clutching his heart.

"Tommy, what's wrong," Ava said, reaching across for his hands. "Do you need help?"

Thomas shook his head and pointed out the window at the three people sitting on a park bench on the far side of the park.

"It's my wife. She's come back from the dead."

Ava turned to look at where he was pointing. She saw three people sitting on a park bench—an older man, a teenager, and a young woman with flaming red hair sitting between them.

Yes, these might have been people in the in-between. She had seen a few. But she saw that Hank saw them too.

Still holding onto Thomas' hands, she said, "Tommy, I think you are looking at your granddaughter."

Bursting into tears, Thomas got out of his chair so quickly, it almost tipped over and started rushing out the door. Ava and Hank grabbed his arm.

"Does she know what you look like?" she asked.

"Probably not."

Then let's not be three crazy people rushing at them. Let's walk over and introduce ourselves and see what happens."

Thomas nodded, but Ava could feel him trembling. She was trembling too. Excitement and fear all rolled into one.

THIRTY SIX

E vie and Owen didn't see them coming.

They had laid their heads onto the bench's back and were gazing at the clear blue sky, holding hands and enjoying the moment. It was James who watched three people open the door of the Diner, cross the street, and walk into the park.

A tall, thin woman had her arm around an older man who was looking at James with a laser focus. The other man walking beside them had his hands clenched into a fist.

James stood and started walking towards them. Whoever they were, he needed to find out before they got to Evie. James had made light of Evie's fear, but only to her. He had taken it seriously. There was never a moment he wasn't watching, and now that they were in Doveland, he felt hyper-alert.

Owen and Evie felt James rise and walk to the three people coming towards them. Evie shook, and Owen put his arm around her and kept her with him on the bench. He had seen James confront people before, and unless these people had weapons, they would be fine.

Valerie and Johnny were heading to Your Second Home when they saw Ava, Thomas, and Hank heading towards the park. They were taking their time crossing the street to meet them when they saw the man walking towards their friends.

Valerie's first instinct was to run to help, but Johnny put his hand on her arm and motioned towards the woman and the teenager on the bench.

"Get Grace," Johnny whispered as he started walking directly towards the bench. But slowly, while sending out waves of comfort in front of him.

Evie noticed him, saw the woman turn away, watched James as he held back the three people who had come from the Diner, and realized this was all about her.

The older man was pointing at her. She thought she heard the name Alice, and for a moment, something pinged in her brain. At the same time, Johnny reached them and stuck out his hand, first to Owen.

"Hi, I'm Johnny," and then to Evie, he added, "I think you are the one we are expecting?"

"All of you?" Evie whispered, seeing two women coming from the coffee shop heading their way.

"All of us," Johnny said. "Welcome."

"But why? And how?"

Johnny gestured to the bench, and the three sat back down together. He nodded at the people who had stopped in the middle of the park and gestured to the man who had been pointing.

"Your grandfather told us you were coming."

"That's my grandfather?" Evie said.

"Perhaps we need to fill him in a little," Owen said, wondering how much he should say.

Johnny smiled at him, acknowledging the fear and excitement radiating off the three strangers.

"You're safe here, Alice." He said.

There was that name again. Alice.

"Is that her name?" Owen asked.

"If that's her grandfather, it is."

"Show him the paper, Evie, or Alice, or something," Owen stumbled.

Evie glanced at James, who nodded, and she reached inside her bra, pulled out a slip of paper and gave it to Johnny.

"Yes, that's Thomas' address. You wrote him a note and told him you were coming, and all of us have been helping him get ready. But you don't remember that, do you?"

Evie shook her head, wondering how he could know that. It wasn't just that she didn't know her name was Alice. She could tell he knew more than that.

"I lost my memory. All I had was this slip of paper, so we came here, hoping that would help me remember."

"It's kind of a long story," Owen added.

"Well then, we would all love to hear it, but perhaps first we let you meet your grandfather."

"I've never met him before?" Evie asked.

"No, he didn't even know you existed until he got that note. But keeping him patient while he waited for you has been hard. Perhaps we can take him out of his misery?"

When Evie hesitated, Johnny asked, "Do you want me to explain some of this to him first?"

Evie nodded.

A few moments later, Thomas emerged from the group and walked to the bench where Evie and Owen waited for him.

"You look just like your grandmother, Ann."

Evie took one look at the man in front of her and ran into his arms. She might not remember exactly who she was but recognized someone that loved her, even before he knew her.

"Welcome home," Thomas said. "Johnny said that you call yourself Evie. Do you want us to call you that too?"

"Yes, please," Evie answered.

By then, everyone had gathered around them, and Thomas introduced Ava, Hank, Valerie, and Grace. Evie introduced Owen and James as her found brother and father. No one questioned what she meant. They knew they would hear the story.

It was the ever-practical Grace who spoke up and said, "As lovely as it is out here, let's go inside."

What she didn't add was that they were attracting quite a crowd. But everyone knew what she meant. Evie grabbed Owen's hand. She was still in danger, and here she was making a scene.

"Do you three have a place to stay?" Ava asked.

"Just got here," James said.

"Great, then it's settled. You stay with us. We have a bunkhouse where Thomas is staying while Hank updates his home in your honor, Evie, and there are still two rooms left."

Evie hesitated until Grace added, "They have the safest home in Doveland. No one will find you there if you don't want them to."

"But how do you know we need to be safe?" Evie asked.

"Ah," Johnny said, "That's our part of the story. If we put both our stories together, we might find some of the answers you seek, Evie."

They were making arrangements for James, Owen, and Evie to follow Ava to her home when the school bus stopped, and Lex burst out of the door and ran toward his mother and brother, his backpack flapping as he ran.

"I saw him again!"

He stopped and looked at the three strangers and addressing the woman with the flaming red hair, he added, "He's looking for you, and he's not far away."

THIRTY SEVEN

E vie looked at the boy and wondered how everyone seemed to know much more about what was going on than she did. *What is this town anyway?* she wondered.

"Who is coming this way, and why for me?"

"This is Lex, my brother, and how he knows is going to sound weird. Do you mind if we tell you once we get you to Ava's house? Where's your car?" Johnny asked.

"We were going to get groceries and maybe gas," James said, pointing at his car across the street.

"No need," Ava said, "There's plenty of food at our house, and more will arrive, I assure you. These people love to bring food. If you'll follow me, we are only a few minutes away."

Johnny looked at Evie and realized she still wasn't sure, so he said, "I'll ride with them, so you all go on. If James wants to get gas, this is an excellent time to get it."

James looked over Evie's head at Johnny and wondered who this young man was who understood the situation so well.

Yes, he had been thinking they might just keep driving if they got in the car alone. But James knew that would be foolish. Evie would run forever, and now at least, there were people who could help.

Of course, he thought to himself, *they could be who Evie is running from, not to, but I don't think so.*

James saw the way Evie's grandfather hugged her. And the kindness in everyone's eyes. Besides, what else could they do? Yes, this was the place to take a stand.

"Would love to have you, young man. You can sit in the back with Evie." James chuckled to himself. He knew the look that Johnny had given Evie. It was the same look he had given his wife the moment he met her. It was one of recognition that this was the one, whether or not he wanted it to be.

Evie was too overwhelmed to have seen it, but one day she would, and James decided that he wanted to be there when it happened. Yes, Evie had found her grandfather, and even if they found a father that loved her, he would still be a found and chosen father.

As Owen sat in the passenger seat, he looked over his shoulder at Evie and Johnny in the back seat and back to James. He winked. They both smiled. This would be fun to watch.

"Let's go, Dad," Owen said.

In the back seat, Evie couldn't help but smile. She had a brother, a father, and now a grandfather, and a town that wanted to embrace her. Who would have thought that this would all happen the day she woke up inside her sleeping bag alone and missing her life?

Whatever her life had been, this was promising to be a very good one.

That's what Evie said to herself. It helped. Because despite all that, the fear that had stalked her before had become a full-blown terror.

· · · ● · ● · · ·

Duke woke up with a massive headache. He knew he brought them on himself. But he couldn't stop working, could he? Besides, he loved his work. Didn't he?

If he were at home, any of his homes, he would have remedies at hand. Treatments that often made the next headache worse, but took care of the present problem.

Not here. Not in this ridiculous hotel in this absurd state. He hated Pennsylvania. He'd always hated it. It was why he didn't have a home here, not even a cabin in the woods like the ones in Montana and Idaho.

But there was nothing he could do but wait it out. It would pass in time. But the headache left him wide open to anyone who was looking for him or watching for him. He couldn't ask for help because that would show his weakness, and weakness was like opening a hole in the dam. All that he had done could slowly leak out, eventually making the hole bigger and bigger until everything he had built would be destroyed.

The problem was, there was already a hole in the dam. That girl, Alice. She had to be stopped, and anyone helping her, because they would ask questions, and another hole would open. He didn't want to waste any more of his life plugging holes.

The more Duke thought about it, the more his head hurt. He couldn't go anywhere, and he had to trust that the meek defenses he could muster were enough to keep him safe for now. Missing the ability to do what usually came so easily to him was torture. But the only way out was to wait.

Duke pulled the pillow over his head and tried to sleep, even though he knew what would happen. He would end up in his past because he wouldn't be able to stop it. There was nothing to do but let the memories come back. They were just memories, nothing he couldn't survive. The sooner he let go, the sooner he would be free to do what he needed to do. Alice could wait one more day. He knew where she was going.

As he fell into sleep and his past, he thought to himself that perhaps this was for the better anyway. He was sure Leo had figured out where his daughter was going by now. Maybe Leo could take care of his daughter the same way he had taken care of his wife. Yes, Duke knew about that. He knew everything about the people who worked for him.

Duke decided that was the life raft he would hold on to for now. And it could happen that way. Then all he had to do was take care of Leo. That would be much easier than Leo imagined, if he ever thought about it. Leo probably thought he was safe. After all, he had never met Duke Quinn in person.

Duke groaned as sleep came for him. Here we go, he thought, as he returned to his childhood and the terror that waited for him there.

THIRTY EIGHT

A ce had to keep looking at the map, which meant sometimes he had to pull off the road to see it.

How in the world did anyone drive before GPS? he wondered.

Luckily or unluckily, the roads had become more rural, which meant pulling off to the side didn't mean having to dodge streams of traffic hurtling by. Ace wished he could remember the road names and directions so he didn't have to keep looking, but he only managed to keep one name and one direction in his head at a time.

Probably the result of getting used to having immediate access to anything. He had forgotten how to memorize anything.

He had been so busy trying to figure out where he was going that it wasn't until he pulled off into a rest stop that he recognized the niggling feeling that something was wrong. He glanced behind him as he walked into the restroom but saw nothing to worry about. Still, the more he thought about it, the more he felt the sensation that someone was watching him. The only person he knew that could care about where he was would be Leo. But he had been sure not to leave any way for Leo to track him.

Ace told himself to stop worrying. He would go into Doveland, find Alice, and explain to her he was on her side. Now anyway.

Maybe he had been all along but couldn't admit it to himself. After all, he hadn't met her before Leo hired him, and Leo was terrifying.

Ace put money into the vending machine, punched in the numbers first for a bag of chips, then a Mars bar. In the drink machine, he bought a can of soda.

Lunch of champions, he said to himself. *Fat, sugar, caffeine, chocolate. All good.*

He stood in the rest stop lobby as he ate his chips and gazed out into the parking lot. A car caught his eye. Unlike most men, he was not into cars. Video games were his thing. Cars just got you somewhere. So he couldn't be sure, but he thought he had seen the black sedan before. But then how many of them were there?

Looking around the lot, he realized it was the only one. Remaining calm, Ace finished his chips and crumbled the bag before throwing it into the trash. He turned to look at the map hanging on the wall as he ate his Mars bar. Doveland was a tiny dot, and he wasn't that far away.

But if he was right, and that car was following him, there was no way he was going to lead it straight into Doveland. He hoped that the person driving didn't know where he was going and was counting on Ace leading him there. How they tracked him down wasn't important right now. What was important was not taking them to Alice.

But if he turned around and went back, they would know that he knew, and then he'd be running. No, it would work better if he kept going. Ace looked at the map again and saw a town on the way to Doveland. Concourse. He would stop there as if that was the place. He'd have to protect himself once he got there because Leo—he assumed it was Leo—would not hesitate to do whatever it took to get information from him.

He stuffed the last bite in his mouth, tossed the wrapper, bought another can of soda, and headed to his car, looking as if he had nothing on his mind. But he did. He had a plan. He hoped it would work.

• • • ●• ● •• •

The thing is, Leo thought. *I am always the smartest person in the room. Too bad for Ace that he didn't remember that.*

It had been easy to follow Ace since he had seen him at the motel. Even when Ace pulled off to look at the map, all Leo did was pass him, pull over somewhere he couldn't be seen, and then wait for him to go by. He stayed a few cars behind him most of the time in case Ace looked in the rear-view mirror.

Now he knew Ace had figured it out. But too late. Because while Ace was in the bathroom, he had placed one of his trackers on the car, just in case.

But he kept on following him, because now that Ace knew, if he didn't follow him, Ace might figure out what he had done.

Instead, he'd let him lead him where he knew Alice probably wasn't. A town called Concourse. Leo wasn't sure what Ace would do. Would he pretend that Alice was there and start searching for her? Or would he try to slip off into the night? That was what Leo assumed Ace would do.

So Leo noted the motel that Ace pulled into and went to the next one down the road. Once again, close enough that it looked like he still needed to follow Ace.

Leo registered, ordered a pizza from the place next door, and went to his room. He needed to rest. If Ace went somewhere, he would know. But Leo knew Ace would stay put. He'd want to make Leo believe that Alice was here in Concourse. Leo figured he could get a good night's sleep while Ace fretted about what to do next.

After checking his messages and telling his assistant one more time that he was on vacation and to take care of anyone who called—yes even "that guy" as his assistant called him—Leo turned off the lights and lay back on the bed.

He was excited. He was sure he would see his daughter soon. It would be a lovely reunion.

THIRTY NINE

While Leo thought about his daughter, his daughter thought about him. Not him, per se. She didn't remember Leo, only that she had a father. Well, of course she did. Everyone had a father. What she remembered was having a father. Vaguely. He was big. She was small.

Again, of course, she was a child. He was a grown man. She remembered that they were both wet, and he was hugging her and whispering her name. The name is what triggered the memory. She had heard the name Alice, and that brought back echoes of her life. As she lay there, she wondered if her father loved her. If he did, why had he never brought her and her mother to Doveland to meet her grandfather?

Her grandfather. She had a grandfather, and he was sleeping just a room away. So were Owen, James, and the man named Hank. Before saying goodnight, Ava had explained all the security present in their house and on their property.

When Evie had asked why, Ava had said that the explanation was for another time, it was a long story. But all Evie needed to know was that they were prepared to protect her. They were good at it.

Evie yawned. She was exhausted. She was safe. At least as safe as she could be. But she kept running through all that had happened that day, meeting Thomas, Tommy—her grandfather—and hearing about her mother and how she had run away.

And then her grandfather had shown her a picture of his wife, Ann. Yes, she looked exactly like her. It was amazing. They could be twins.

Then he showed her a picture of her mother, Maggie. Maggie didn't have the flaming hair. She looked more like her dad—with curly brown hair and blue eyes, but not the vibrant blue of her grandmother's eyes and hers.

She knew that everyone hoped her memory would come back if she looked at that picture, but it didn't. Nothing. It was as if there was a wall between her and her memories. Fear had built it. Not fear of what would happen, but fear of the memory of what had happened. That much she had figured out.

James and Owen had done most of the talking for her while she picked at the food that Ava's friends had brought. It was delicious. She just wasn't hungry. Finally, they stopped asking her questions, and her grandfather had talked. That's when he showed her pictures. She was grateful for his stories and wished she could feel something about them.

Where was her mother? Thomas didn't know. Why hadn't she come home? Thomas didn't know. No one knew. But she did, she knew that she did—she just couldn't remember.

After they ate, the woman who owned the coffee shop asked Evie if she had questions.

She had laughed. Oh yes, she had a million questions. Not just about who she was and why she couldn't remember, but about who they all were. And most of all, what did that boy mean when he said, "He's on his way." Who was on his way, and how did he know that?

She could tell that they were trying to answer the question without freaking her out. But it didn't help. Not because she didn't believe them. But because she did.

When they explained that a few of them, including the boy, Lex, could do something called remote viewing, she froze. Literally. It felt as if someone had thrown a bucket of ice water on her. She couldn't breathe.

Ava had seen her reaction and immediately wrapped her in a blanket and started whispering that everything would be all right. There was nothing to fear.

Afterward, Evie had said thank you, and how did Ava know what to do?

Ava and her husband, Evan, had glanced at each other and then said, "children." Evie thought they were trying to tell her they were used to comforting people who were afraid because they had children, but she knew it was more than that.

Someday maybe she would hear the story if she stayed alive long enough, because that was what she had realized when she heard about remote viewing. She remembered it. She knew about it, and she knew that was how people knew where she was. Except for one thing. She had lost her memory, but she had not lost the ability to cloak herself.

It felt like it had been a habit so long that she had kept it up, and now she knew that had saved her life. That was why they hadn't found her yet, whoever they were. But Lex said they were coming.

"Who," they had all asked. "More than one man," he had answered and then said he was sorry he couldn't see more.

"That's enough, Lex," his mother, Valerie, had said. "It has given us information. Now you have to stop it."

After seeing Evie's reaction, Lex had gone pale, and his brother, Johnny, had put his arm around him and whispered something. All the time they had been talking, Johnny had not taken his eyes

161

off of her. Sometimes he looked at her directly. Other times, she just knew he was keeping her in his peripheral vision.

Despite herself, Evie had been flattered. It had felt wonderful when James and Owen had told her she looked beautiful, but this was different. It wasn't just what she looked like. He saw something else, and that something else was what she wanted to find again.

Finally, Evie felt sleep creeping around her consciousness, so before she fell asleep she thought of each of her new friends and thanked them.

At the last minute, she could have sworn she saw the person Thomas had said was her mother. But it was hazy, and Evie figured she was just remembering the picture she had seen.

Her mother was either alive, or she was dead, but either way, she couldn't be standing in her room.

FORTY

E vie woke to the sun streaming through the window and the sound of someone laughing. Outside the window, she could see Ben running around the yard chasing Owen. Then Owen chased Ben.

How did Owen make friends so easily, she wondered?

After dressing, Evie joined everyone in the kitchen where Ava was feeding people as they got up. She was the last one.

"I'm so sorry for sleeping in," Evie said. "You don't have to make me breakfast!"

"Still have pancake batter and didn't want to throw it away, so please let me use it up," Ava said as she tapped on the window and signaled for Ben to come in.

"Where is everyone?" Evie asked, trying not to moan with pleasure at how good the pancakes tasted.

"Hank and Thomas went to the house to see how the construction is going. They took James with them because he said he would love to help. Your grandfather's house was sadly out of date, and Tommy wanted it to be ready for you.

"He didn't tell you last night how depressed he had become until he got your letter. To his credit, he picked himself up, came into

163

the Diner, and met Barbara, Pete, and Hank. From there, the rest is history, even though it was less than a week ago."

"Do you all always take on people like Thomas and me and Owen and James?"

Ava paused. "Yes, we do. It's something we believe in. It's the idea that people find each other in their different lifetimes. Kurt Vonnegut made up a word for it. He called it a karass."

"Do you think we are part of this karass of yours?"

"I do," Ava said.

Evie put her dishes in the dishwasher and then leaned against the counter. Owen had gone back into the bunkhouse. Ben was in his room, getting ready for school. Ava waited for the next question.

"Are evil people part of a karass, too."

"Not in Vonnegut's definition. He said karasses gather to do God's purpose."

"So, how do evil people fit into this?"

"Maybe the question is, why are they evil?" Ava answered. "Some people do bad things, not knowing any better, or thinking they have no other choice. Once they discover the truth, they stop doing bad and chose good. You will find these people inside our karass. They are the best good people I know."

Ava held up her hand when Evie started to ask who.

"Right now, who they are doesn't matter. Stick around long enough, and you will hear their stories. They woke up. They got, and took, their second chance."

"And others? The ones that do bad because they enjoy it?"

"Do you know people like this, Evie?" Ava asked as gently as she could.

"I think I do. Do you?"

"We have met them."

"And?"

"Remember this, Evie. Good always, always, always wins over the intent of evil."

"Always?"

"Always."

Neither woman said anything. Ava was thinking of the evil she had known and the good that governed her life now.

Evie was wondering what kind of evil was searching for her because she was sure that it was.

"I'm heading to yoga. Would you like to come with me?" Ava asked.

"Sometime, yes, I would. But I wonder if you could tell me about the bike trail I saw running along the road. Does it go all the way from that town we went through to get to Doveland?"

"It's lovely, isn't it," Ava said. "Hank's construction company, and Johnny and a crew of teenagers learning construction built it."

"Another story?" Evie asked.

"Definitely!"

Seeing Evie's face, Ava added, "We have lots of bikes. Do you want to take one and try out the trail? You can access it at the bottom of our driveway."

Fifteen minutes later, Evie was riding the trail by herself. Owen wanted to walk the other way into Doveland. Evie said she would ride to Concourse and then come back to have lunch with him.

Ava gave them each an untraceable phone with numbers already programmed into it. She told them that she expected them both to answer when she called to check up on them.

They both laughed, and Owen said, "Yes, mother," which only made tears come into Ava's eyes as she smiled at them both. Yes, she loved collecting people.

She had told Evie that there was a tracker on the bike, just in case, and gave her one to slip into her pants' pocket.

She had also given her a jacket she said belonged to her daughter, Hannah.

When Evie asked where Hannah was, Ava shook her head.

"At her real home."

At Evie's puzzled expression, Ava had answered, "If I told you where Hannah is now, you'd really think we were weird. Let's leave that for later. Much later."

Later that morning, when Evie got warm, she took the jacket off and tied it around her waist, and saw a ladybug sewed inside. She figured it was a secret message to Hannah and smiled.

She was grateful that no one had said it wasn't wise for her to be biking by herself. She needed this time alone. She felt like herself riding the path out in nature, moving her legs. All that time in the car had taken a toll.

She knew that Ava had done everything she could to make her feel safe, and she was also grateful for that. A few hours' bike ride to Concourse, and she'd turn around and meet Owen in the park. Then they could decide where to go for lunch.

What Evie didn't know was how hard it was for Ava to watch her bike away. Yes, she had their phones. Yes, she had given Owen and Evie trackers, but as a mother, she couldn't stop worrying.

Throughout yoga, Ava kept reminding herself that all was well. It helped—a little.

FORTY ONE

Owen started walking to town, turned around, and came back to the house.

Ava had gone, but Evan was in his office. When Owen explained what he needed, Evan clapped him on the back and then gave him a hug which threw Owen off balance.

These people accepted him without question, and his parents threw him out because he was different?

Evan gave Owen his bike since they were about the same height. A fanny pack and helmet hung on the bar, just as Evie's had, and Owen put both on, hoping he remembered how to ride a bike.

He rode it cautiously down the driveway toward the road. But once he got to the bike path, he was no longer afraid. Confident of his skills, Owen started peddling as fast as he could. After a few minutes, he realized he couldn't keep that pace, so he slowed enough until he could breathe properly.

He hoped that Evie was riding slowly so he could catch up. He didn't want her to know that he was right behind her. He knew she wanted time to herself, and he planned to give that to her, but at the same time, it didn't feel right not watching out for her.

The bike path had a walking trail beside it. Owen smiled at the planning. That meant he didn't have to watch out for walkers, or they for him. There weren't that many bikers, so it was easy to avoid them. He called out "hey" as he passed, and people said "hey" back—all smiles.

I'm going to love living here, Owen thought. *I'm sure there is a pizza shop here where I could get a job.*

He hoped Evie and James would stay, too. Maybe they could get a house together, and he'd have an actual family. And friends.

All these pleasant thoughts and plans for the future occupied Owen's mind as he peddled as quickly as he could to get Evie in his sights. But she was nowhere to be seen.

He thought that Evie was probably enjoying the freedom of moving and zipping along. He tried not to worry too much. He'd find her in Concourse, and they could ride back together. Once he got to Concourse he'd call her. Like it or not, Evie was stuck with a brother that worried too much.

• • • ● • ● • • •

Owen was right. Once Evie felt how good it was to move, she started going faster. It pleased her that her breath was steady, and her legs felt like pistons. It was such a delightful feeling. Not only the physical sensation, but also the awareness that she was doing something that she loved to do, back when she knew herself.

It was an extraordinarily beautiful fall day. The trees along the path were decked out in their best fall finery. The red maples were living up to their name with their deep red leaves backlit by the sun, looking as if they were on fire. Other maples were dressed in a range of colors, from gold to burgundy. Oak leaves still hung on the tree but had changed to a dark copper.

All were interspersed with evergreens and wildflowers along the sides of the paths. She named them to herself as she rode. Queen Ann's lace, Purple Asters, and Joe Pye Weed.

How was she now remembering these plant names when she didn't remember her life? She knew it was because they didn't carry fear. Last night she had realized that although she didn't know what had caused her to lose her memory in the first place, it was not what was keeping it from coming back. It was fear.

That's partly what this ride was about. Evie hoped to shake off the fear. Find freedom in being on her own. Maybe doing something that felt so good would shake loose what was scaring her, and she could face it and then do something about it.

Time flew by, and before she knew it, Evie had made it to the end of the official bike path. Ahead of her, she could see the town's traffic circle, almost like the one in Doveland, but she thought not as pretty.

Still, she decided she could use a break before heading back to Doveland and lunch. She had spotted a Dairy Queen and remembered she liked their soft ice cream. That would fuel her return trip.

She was so delighted that she remembered that she liked the ice cream at the Dairy Queen, and feeling the adrenalin of the bike ride, Evie didn't notice the man standing on the corner.

But he saw her.

Leo couldn't believe it. He had to look again to be sure. It had been two years since she had left home. They had hugged, and he had brushed back her hair from her eyes and told her to visit often. She had looked right back into his eyes and calmly replied that she would.

What a liar. She had never come home again. She had attended school, but all on line. She had never shown up at the job she claimed to have. It had all been lies.

Using up a few favors, he had tracked her down. And then told Ace to do what he needed to do to find what Alice had taken. Ace had not.

Instead, Leo knew that Ace had followed Alice down the rabbit hole and lost himself.

It was ironic that Ace was still back at the motel while Leo had come to town to get some coffee. The coffee at the motel was god-awful. And there, without any effort on his part, was the object of his search.

He had seen her ride into town, but it wasn't until she parked at the Dairy Queen and took off her helmet that he was sure. Her hair was shorter, but it was still flaming red. He had been so proud of his daughter when she was young. He showed her off everywhere.

"My beautiful daughter, Alice," he'd say. "Yes, I am raising her on my own. Her beloved mother died in an accident. It's only by the grace of God that Alice didn't perish too."

People would smile and coo at Alice. But anyone who knew him recognized the icy glint in his eyes. Still, they chose to believe him. Sometimes he even believed it himself. He was the best father a girl could ever want.

Until she left him.

Now, after all this time, here they were in a strange town, brought together by unseen forces. It was fate. He had her in his sights. He'd let her eat her ice cream first.

I might as well give her one last good memory before I take back what is mine.

Then Alice looked his way.

FORTY TWO

Johnny was redoing his mother's business website. He had set it up for her before, but she was adding additional services and products. Besides, it looked a little outdated. It needed an update, and he was the man to do it.

When his mom opened up the design studio in her house instead of running a bed-and-breakfast, he and Lex were skeptical. What did their mom know about design and business? Even though her friend Mandy had helped set it up, and was her partner, they were still worried.

Their father, Harold, had died, and his death started the unraveling of his and Dr. Joe's past. No one had known. Even his new step-father, Craig, had not suspected that the man who sold him his medical practice had been a serial murderer.

As a teenager, his dad had helped hide some of Dr. Joe's secrets. Johnny understood how that could have happened. Not that long ago, he had fallen for the same set of lies, and if his mother's friends hadn't rescued him from the path he was taking, he would have done what his father did.

So he didn't hate his father for it. None of them did. They understood, including his mother. Instead, she concentrated on what Harold had done for her that made her happy.

She told her sons that there were many reasons she was grateful that she had married their dad. The most precious gift of all is he had given her Lex and Johnny. And then he had moved them to Doveland and bought them their house. She said she could go on and on with the good he had done for all three of them.

But she was also grateful for being free. Now she could choose how to live her life. And discovering that she loved running a small design business was liberating. Although she had loved teaching and being the school's principal, this was what she wanted to do now.

But designing websites was not on her list of things she loved to do or wanted to learn, so she had asked Johnny to learn about it. To the astonishment of both of them, he loved doing it. So while he was in school, he switched his major to business and started taking computer design and marketing courses. He had found his calling.

The school was close enough to Doveland that he often came home and helped his mother with her business. He planned to branch out from there. Valerie had questioned him repeatedly, wanting to know if he was sure.

"Don't do it because of me, Johnny," she would say, and he promised he wasn't. Not really. He knew she would be fine without him.

Craig was a wonderful man, and he was happy to call him dad. And they had amazing friends. Lex was doing great in school, so they didn't need him to come home.

No, he wanted to come back to Doveland for himself. It was what called him. He could help businesses all over the world from his computer.

Why live away from the support system that Doveland offered him, he had asked himself.

Because that's what it did. He was weird in the worldview's eyes. Only in Doveland did the weirdness feel like a gift rather than a burden or something to hide.

He could do things most people couldn't. Sometimes he didn't like it. Other times he was grateful for what he could do.

He had loved helping Rachel and Byran with the woman who had died and then went back in time to fix her mistake. Only the people directly involved remembered that part. Everyone else thought Connie Matthews's life had been what it looked like all along.

It had been thoroughly satisfying. Life in Doveland was good. He had no desire for something else.

And then yesterday, that girl turned and looked at him, and everything stopped. He had heard of love at first sight, but thought it was a bunch of nonsense.

Yes, he had girlfriends, but once he got to know them, he knew they would never understand who he was or what he could do without making a big deal of it one way or another.

So he had decided to be a single guy. He was young. He had work, family, and a town he loved. Then the girl with the flaming red hair and searing blue eyes came to town. He smiled as he updated yet another web page and decided he would go out to Ava's later that morning and make sure everything was okay.

Sure, no other motive there, buddy, he said to himself.

A moment later, a wave of dizziness passed over him. He knew what was coming. The room darkened around him as if somewhere else opened up inside his mind.

That was the only way he could ever describe it to anyone. He had long ago given up caring how it happened. It just did. And what he saw made him jump up and brace himself on the desk.

He saw Owen racing along the bike path towards Concourse. He saw Evie standing in front of a Dairy Queen. He saw a man watching her.

Johnny started running. He grabbed the car keys and burst out the door. He knew he'd never make it in time. The closest person was Owen.

He reached out to Owen and said, "go faster." He hoped that Owen would think it was his own thoughts and not freak out, knowing it was someone else in his head.

The vision faded. Johnny drove as fast as he could. He called Hank.

Hank didn't ask why when Johnny said, "Dairy Queen, Concourse." He just ran to his car and started driving.

Thomas and James had called after him, but he knew they would slow him down. Hank knew a back way to Concourse. After all, it was his hometown. It was where he learned to be a bad guy. If it were necessary, he would be one again.

Whatever Johnny wanted him to do, he would do. And he would see it as a good thing.

FORTY THREE

Ace slept in. He didn't think that he had. When he rolled over in bed to check the time, he thought only a few hours had passed. When he saw the time and glimpsed sunlight through the slit between the curtains, he bolted out of bed, swearing under his breath.

He slipped on his pants and, without bothering to put his shoes on, stepped outside to see if he could see Leo's car. At first, he didn't, so he walked into the parking lot, shielding his eyes from the blazing sun. He heaved a sigh of relief when he saw that the car was still there.

You're an idiot, he mumbled to himself as he walked back to his room, only to find the door closed and, of course, locked.

Leaning his forehead on the door frame, he swore at himself and then remembered that he had left one key in his pants pocket the night before when he had gone out to get a soda and snacks from the vending machine.

At the time, he had berated himself for eating junk food for dinner again, but now he was momentarily grateful for his careless ways.

And that's what I am being, Ace said to himself. *Careless. I shouldn't have let myself sleep in.*

What if Leo had figured out that Alice was in Doveland and gone there already? What if, after rushing all this way to help Alice, he had been sleeping when she needed help?

Ace knew he had to calm himself down and get on with his plan. It didn't matter it was late in the morning, Leo was still at the motel, and it seemed that Leo would wait for him to make the next move.

Yes, he knew that Leo had put a tracker on his car. How else had he ended up being in the same place? It was a game of cat and mouse that they were playing. He was the mouse. But mice often outwitted the cat, and that was precisely what he was going to do.

After a hot shower, followed by a blast of cold water for thirty seconds to wake him up, Ace stood in front of the foggy pealing mirror and did his best to give himself a clean shave. He needed a haircut, and he needed more sleep, but it was the best he could do.

He would see Alice today. But he wasn't planning on driving to Doveland. He had seen a bike shop in town, and that was how he'd get there. He'd leave the room looking as if he was coming back.

Ace knew that somehow Leo would get in the room to make sure that Ace hadn't left. He doubted it would fool Leo for long, but all he needed was time to warn Alice and tell her he was on her side.

Because that was it. He was on her side. He was done with this shady stuff that Leo was into. Ace knew that in choosing sides, he was putting himself at risk. Not only would Leo want to get rid of him, but any of his clients that would find out about it would join Leo in that desire.

Ace didn't fool himself into thinking he would get the girl and live happily ever after. He planned on turning himself in and convincing Alice to go into witness protection with him. He doubted she would do that, but Ace was sure he had enough information that he could make that deal. But first, he needed Alice.

A few minutes later, Ace was on his way to the bike shop. He had made sure no one saw him leave the room wearing a hat and sunglasses. Walking behind buildings wherever he could in case Leo was watching the road, Ace moved as quickly as he could toward town. The sooner he was heading to Doveland, the better he would feel.

Rounding the last corner, he could see the bike shop across the road. He looked both ways before crossing, took a few steps, and then backed up. A woman was standing outside the Dairy Queen with flaming red hair. She was looking the other way, but how many people had hair like that?

Ace's heart raced. He could talk to her now. All he had to do was figure out a way not to scare her before he had a chance to explain himself.

But then Ace saw what Alice was looking at. Not what, who. Leo saw Ace at the same moment that Ace saw him, which caused both of them to hesitate.

Evie looked behind her to see what her father was looking at, saw Ace, and without thinking, started running. She had no idea where to run to, and if she had been thinking, she would have taken her bike. But there was no time.

All she could think of was, get away from these two men.

She knew who they were. She barely registered that since she knew who they were, her memory had returned, and along with it, the memory of why she had been hiding.

She had something that they wanted, and now she remembered what it was and why she had been going to her grandfather's.

She had decided that she had nowhere else to turn. Her mother had told her stories of what her grandfather did for a living and how kind and smart he was.

Evie remembered asking her mother why she had run away. Her mother said she had chosen the wrong path and ended up with her father, and she never wanted Leo to know who her father was or how to find him.

"Why?" little Alice had asked.

Her mother hadn't answered. Maybe one day she would have told her, but she never had a chance. Because as she ran, Evie remembered the most terrible thing of all.

Her father had killed her mother, so she could tell no one what she knew. But her father wasn't as smart as he thought. Maggie had hidden the information where she knew that her grown-up daughter would eventually find it. And she had.

FORTY FOUR

Duke Quinn groaned. He was having a nightmare. Chaos was all around him. Except he wasn't sleeping. He had been awake for the last few hours. The headache had faded away until all he felt was exhausted.

But he had been in bed too long, so he dragged himself to the one chair in the living room, thinking it was bloody uncomfortable.

He wondered why he hadn't gotten a suite instead of this room. He had more money than God. What was his problem? At least he would have a comfortable chair.

Or not, he thought. *Money didn't always buy comfort.* He could attest to that. He had money, and he was unhappy and uncomfortable.

How had it gotten to this point? he wondered. It was time to stop. He would get rid of Leo and his daughter and then be done with his work. He would stop everything. He didn't need more money. He needed peace and quiet.

With that thought, Duke had been content for a moment. Only a moment. And then the nightmare began. Duke hated it when this happened, when he had no control over the experience.

Instead, the outside world dimmed, and he was in the middle of the street with cars and trucks going through him.

Even though he wasn't really there, the fear of watching something come at you was as real as if you were. He forced himself to step out of the street and onto the sidewalk. Calming himself, he slowed his breathing down and looked around.

Remote viewing is like dreaming, often hazy and disjointed. Duke didn't know where he was, but he knew who he was looking at. Leo.

Leo was looking at his daughter. The two of them exchanged looks. Then she looked behind her, and Duke saw her recognize the other man. He didn't know who he was, but she did. And that's when the viewing shut down.

As Duke rushed to shower and dress, he wondered where they were. It wasn't Doveland. He knew what Doveland looked like, and it couldn't have changed that much since he had been gone.

Whatever, Duke thought. *They'll end up in Doveland, and I'll be waiting. I'll finish them all off, and then it will be over. For good.*

. . . . ● . ● . . .

A bird's-eye view of what was happening in Concourse would have revealed Hank and Johnny in their cars, and Owen on his bike—all converging into the center of town while Leo, Ace, and Evie were running away from it.

But the people who watched what happened from the stores and the street didn't see all of that. They saw a young man chasing after an older man and dragging him to the ground, where a quick fight took place.

Before anyone could stop it, the older man overpowered the young man and, while he was lying still on the sidewalk, kicked him in the ribs and the head, and then ran the direction he had been going before the young man had tackled him.

A few seconds later, a car pulled up to the sidewalk, and the driver said he would take the man lying on the sidewalk to the hospital.

"Do you know him?" they had asked.

The driver said yes, and they helped him put the injured man in the car. The driver circled the square and headed back toward Doveland, but not before stopping beside a boy on a bike. A moment later, both the bike and the boy were in the car, too.

But later, when they thought of that morning, not one of them remembered what had happened.

What none of them had seen was a woman with flaming red hair turn when the young man called out "stop." But not to her.

To her, he yelled, "Run, Alice."

And when she heard Ace yell "run," it shocked her enough to stop running. She turned in time to see the two men fighting on the sidewalk.

At the same time, Hank pulled up beside her and told her to get in. As they pulled away, Evie saw Leo kick Ace and leave him lying still on the sidewalk.

"We need to help him," Evie said as Hank headed back to Doveland.

"Not stopping," Hank said. "We need to get you to safety."

For a moment, Evie hesitated. She had been running from Ace too. Why help him? She could just let him lie there. Hank was right. She needed to get to safety.

But Ace had protected her. Whatever he had been doing before, he had been there for her at that moment.

Hank looked at Evie and realized she would not let it alone. "Johnny will get him."

Moments later she heard Johnny in her head say, "Got him and Owen. Meet us at Ava's. We'll call Craig."

"Johnny's calling Craig, and he wants us to meet at Ava's."

Hank looked over at Evie, wondering, as he did every so often, how he had ever gotten mixed up with this bunch of people who could do the things they did.

Instead, he asked, "You remembered?"

"I remembered," Evie confirmed. "And now I have gotten you all into trouble."

Hank laughed.

"We've been there before. It will work out."

Evie smiled at Hank and knew he thought that it would. But she doubted they had ever dealt with what she had coming after her, and now them.

She had shut down what Duke Quinn was seeing, but that wouldn't stop him for long.

Now both her father and Duke were going to Doveland, and neither one of them would quit before they got what they wanted. No one would get in their way.

But Evie also knew she would do whatever she had to do to protect these people—including letting herself be caught. She just hoped that it didn't come to that.

In her mind, she heard Johnny say, "It won't," and she smiled in spite of herself.

FORTY FIVE

Ava's phone vibrated. Usually, she kept it off in her yoga bag, but today, she couldn't shake the feeling that something would go wrong and kept it by her mat. She wasted no time in picking up the phone to check the message.

It was short. "Get James and Thomas and take them to the house."

As quietly as she could, she gathered her things and smiled at Emily so she wouldn't worry. There was nothing that Emily could do, and there was no reason to drag her into what was happening.

As Ava walked to her car, she took in the beautiful view from Emily's Hill. The view of Doveland always took her breath away. She loved this town and these people.

On the way to town, Ava called Grace and asked Grace to come to her house. At first she debated calling. Did they need to drag everyone into it? Or was it a protective move? Once she decided it was for Grace's protection, the decision was simple. And Grace would know if anyone else needed to be there too.

Within fifteen minutes of the text from Hank, she was in front of Thomas' house, where he and James were pacing frantically back and forth on the sidewalk. They were in her car almost before she came to a stop.

No one said anything. None of them knew what was going on. All of them were afraid of what the answers might be if they asked the question.

James and Thomas both breathed a sigh of relief when they saw Evie step out of Hank's truck.

However, instead of running towards them, she stood at the truck, afraid to move. Now that she remembered everything, she was more terrified than she had been before.

Now she knew what she had gotten these two men into, and she shouldn't have. She should have disappeared instead.

But being rushed by both men, and then Owen, as he tumbled out of Evan's car, broke down her defenses, and she started sobbing, which scared the men more than her frozen state.

Evan and Hank lifted Ace out of the car and headed into the house.

Ava waited until Grace arrived along with Valerie before ushering everyone else who was standing in the parking lot inside. She had seen Craig's car, so she knew he was already there. He had a key to their house, as did all their circle. It was the safe place for everyone.

Ava debated whether she should get Ben from school, but decided to wait until she knew what was going on and who was in danger—all of them, or only Evie?

· · · ● · ● · · ·

Leo stopped running. He walked casually, checked out a few store windows, even bought a cup of coffee from a cart. It was surprisingly good.

When no police sirens were heading to town, or people coming after him, he went back to the motel. Although glad there had been no police, he knew it was because someone had blocked everyone's memories of what had happened.

Yes, it had happened quickly, but people had phones, and they used them. That someone had that kind of ability to stop all that was terrifying. He knew only one man who did, and if he was around, he might as well start digging his own grave. And if it wasn't him, then who was it?

However, Leo was used to compartmentalizing problems, and that one was one he couldn't solve right now. So, instead, he did what Ace knew Leo would do. He searched Ace's room. After finding nothing that would help him, he went back to his room, where he first showered and shaved before packing.

Leo had seen Alice, and she had run from him, her father. Which meant she knew what he wanted.

It gave him a strange sense of pride knowing that this woman that eluded him for so long was his daughter. She was smart and capable, more intelligent than most people he went after.

Of course, she was the first person he had to eliminate for himself and not a client. Well, not the first person. Her mother was the first.

But if his clients ever found about the records he kept about who and what he did, and for whom, he would be a dead man. But not until after they tortured him into telling them where he had hidden the information.

And that would be even worse because he didn't have those old records anymore. He hadn't since Maggie had died.

If only he had known that she had taken them before he made that accident happen. Later, he had hoped that she had the information with her when she died, and that all of it was buried forever in the lake.

But then, one day, Alice had stopped looking at him with love in her eyes, and he knew she had discovered his secret.

He knew that no daughter would want an assassin for a father, but what could he do about that? It's what he was. No, he didn't use guns. He hated them. If a weapon was necessary, he hired someone else. No, his way was subtle and untraceable. It always looked like an accident or ill health. It was that ability that had attracted the big man himself.

He should have said no. But he was flattered, and his ego took over. Something he hated about himself now. He tried never to let emotion rule his decisions, and he was a master at it.

After all, he was not letting emotions keep him from stopping Alice. But he had taken pride in his work, and that a man like Duke Quinn wanted to hire him stoked the flames of his ego, and he had said yes.

It was the worst decision of his life. At the time, he didn't know that, though. He didn't know anything other than that the powerful man who started Quinn Enterprises and ran it quietly behind the scenes thought he good enough and trustworthy enough to hire. Once Duke Quinn started giving him assignments, he understood how Duke had become so powerful.

Leo turned his car towards Doveland. He figured that's where all those people had gone. Yes, they were protecting Alice, so they were now part of the problem. He prided himself on being calm in all situations. And on the outside, that was what he appeared to be. But inside, he was not. Inside he was furious, and if he admitted it to himself, he was also terrified of Duke Quinn.

It pleased him to note, however, that he had been right about Ace. Ace had fallen for his daughter. Who could blame him? After all, he had fallen for Maggie. Yes, Alice was like her mother, but she was also like him. Calculating and extremely capable. That made her quite a danger to him.

First, he had to find her and get the information back before Duke Quinn found him. Because he was sure that Duke was on his way. And what made him even more dangerous was Leo had never seen Duke or even heard his authentic voice. He could be anyone. And he could already be in Doveland.

Leo hoped not. He needed to get there first, deal with Alice and her friends, and then prepare to deal with Duke Quinn after that.

FORTY SIX

"What are we missing?"

It was Grace who asked the question. Ava realized that was why Grace needed to be there. She would cut through all the drama and find the heart of the matter. What were they missing?

They had set Ace up in one of the bedrooms, and Craig was sitting with him to make sure that he didn't have a concussion. Ace kept mumbling that he wanted to see Alice, and finally, Craig had given in and let Evie talk to him, reminding her to keep him as calm as possible.

After Craig promised he would remain outside the door, Evie agreed, but she stood as far away from the bed as possible until she realized that Ace was incapable of moving. And besides, he had tried to save her.

Moving next to the bed, she reached for his hand. Yes, he had fooled her or had tried to. She had realized his intentions almost immediately. So actually, she was the one to blame because she had led him on, hoping to delay the inevitable—her father coming after her. If she could make Ace believe that she would lead him to the information her mother left her, it bought her time.

She hadn't expected to care for him, and now she realized that he hadn't expected to care for her either.

"Thank you for stopping Leo," she finally said.

Ace tried hard not to let the tears in his eyes overflow. He still couldn't believe that he had made that choice. It meant that life as he knew it was over for him.

But then, the moment he had agreed to work for Leo, he had signed his life away. Only then, at the time, it had seemed a fair trade. He had been destined to stay in prison for a long time. He had let his temper get the best of him and pushed someone in a bar who inconveniently died after hitting his head on the edge of a table.

Leo had come to the prison and said he could get him out, but he had to work for him. Forever.

It sounded good to Ace, especially after Leo had shown him a picture of the girl he was supposed to charm enough to become his girlfriend.

What a deal, he had thought. And it had been. Just not the one he had imagined. He should have known that someone powerful enough to get him out of that prison sentence had acquaintances everywhere, all of them now motivated to stop Ace. But did Alice know that?

So that's what he asked her. "It was temporary. Nothing can stop him. You know he has people everywhere, don't you, Alice?"

"I'm not Alice anymore," she said.

Ace turned his head to the side, and Evie could see the bruises on his face. When he looked back, he said, "I don't blame you. Who are you now?"

"Evie Lynn."

Ace tried not to laugh. It hurt too much. "You named yourself after those two guys you like on RuPaul's Drag Race?"

As Ace said that, more of Evie's memory flooded back, filling in gaps, and she remembered. It wasn't just at The Pizza Shop that she had seen the show. She and Ace had watched it together. Not all of their relationship had been a lie.

"OMG," Evie said, sitting down in the chair by the bed and putting her head down beside Ace's hand.

"I'm so sorry," she finally said. "I knew you worked for my father, but then I started to like you, and I realized I needed to get away before it became serious. And I was afraid of you, too."

"You had good reason to be," Ace said. "I was working for your father, but then I started liking you too much, too. Guess I'm really screwed now. And being here is only making it worse for you."

"No, it's not. Nothing will make it worse than it already is, and as soon as we solve this problem, we'll make sure you are safe."

"There's no way you can make that promise ... Evie .... Your father and the men he works for are too powerful. Give him the information he wants, and maybe he will go away."

Evie shook her head. "You know he won't. And even if he left me alone, what about all the people he has hurt and will continue to hurt? You know I have to stop him."

She gestured towards the living room. "Out there, I think there are people who can help. But they need the entire story to do it."

Evie leaned over and kissed Ace on the forehead and said, "Thank you again, Ace."

Squaring her shoulders, she returned to the living room just in time to hear Grace's question, "What are we missing?"

"Quite a bit, it turns out," Evie said. "Now that I remember everything, I know what I have to do."

• • • • • • • • • •

On the opposite side of town, Duke Quinn stood beside the lake and remembered. He remembered things he never wanted to remember. He had wanted to bury his past. He never wanted to remember his life and who he had been.

He had promised himself he would never come back. He promised himself, standing by this lake, that he would build a world that isolated him from all of his past. He wanted to have his past stay missing and never be uncovered by anyone, including himself.

Instead, now he had to drag it all back up. And it was all that man Leo's fault. Leo had taken away his safe life. A life sealed off from painful memories.

In return, he would take away Leo's life and all that he held dear. And at the same time, perhaps take a little revenge on the town that had not protected him from the bullies and his father. Instead, he had to do it himself the way he always had.

What am I missing, Duke Quinn asked himself. *Why was I brought here?*

FORTY SEVEN

Thomas listened to his granddaughter's story with a sinking heart. To his heartbroken question of why Maggie hadn't come home, Evie hesitated before answering.

"Because she was protecting you. Even in the end, we weren't coming here, grandfather, even though that was what she told my father. We were going somewhere Leo could never find us. It was never her intention to harm you.

"I remember her telling me stories about how wonderful you were, but I was never to mention you to my father. And I never did. Not because I understood why I shouldn't, but because I had promised my mother, and it was one of the few memories I had of her.

"Once I found what my mother left me, the only place I could think of going was to you. She told me your name and where you lived. You might not know this, but she loved you. But even though I was coming to you, I tried to protect you the same way that she did.

"I destroyed any way to track me before I left. I hid more cash on the mountain, but of course, when I woke up not remembering who I was, I didn't know that.

"Luckily, I had written your address on that piece of paper. Otherwise, I don't know what would have happened. On the other hand, look at what I have done. The very thing my mother tried to prevent, My father and his cronies finding you.

"I made a huge mistake. I brought all of this mess here to you and this town, and even to Owen and James, who had no idea what they were getting into when they said they would help me."

Looking around at the room, Evie said, "I am so sorry."

It was Owen who stood up and said, "No. No, you can't be sorry. James and I came because we wanted to. You told us you were afraid, we knew something terrible was chasing you, and we chose to come with you. And we would do it again."

From his seat on the couch, James nodded and added, "Wouldn't have missed it for the world."

Thomas stood to hug Evie, saying, "I am so grateful you have come home. It was the right choice. I am sure it's what your mother wanted you to do. You have changed my life. Actually, I believe you have changed more than one person's life by making that choice."

As Thomas hugged Evie, he glanced over her shoulder at Johnny, who blushed and looked down. Everyone pretended that they didn't see it or understand what Thomas had meant, but they knew. Even if Evie didn't know yet, they did.

Grace cleared her throat, and everyone turned to look at her, acknowledging once again that Grace was leading them. Something she would probably deny, but that wouldn't change anything.

"Yes, Evie. Your coming here is a blessing to us. And we are quite capable of taking care of the evil that is chasing you in whatever form that is."

"What do you mean? It's my father. It's who he is and what he does for a living that is the evil. And how evil is a person who would kill his wife and daughter to protect himself?"

"Yes, it's your father. But there is someone else, too."

Evie looked around the room and realized that she was the only one who didn't know what Grace was talking about.

"Someone else? Who? And how do you know?"

It was Johnny who answered her question.

"We know because Lex saw him, told me, and then I saw him too. And the who? We don't know his name. And the why? Because you are Leo's daughter, and you have what he wants."

Evie stared at Johnny, and when he smiled at her, she knew what he meant. He and his brother were remote viewers. She knew about them and had learned from her mother how to block them.

"How did my mother know about remote viewing?" Evie stuttered, not bothering to fill in how she had got to that question. But everyone knew.

A long silence filled the room. A knowing silence, waiting for the one person who could answer to choose to tell the truth.

Finally, Thomas spoke.

"I taught her."

Evie collapsed into the closest chair and stared at the man across the room from her.

The missing pieces of her memory filtering back.

"And now we know what we were missing," Grace said. "The why of it. But there's more, isn't there, Tommy?"

It was both a gentle and a firm request. One Thomas knew he could not refuse. It was time to talk. He hoped it wasn't too late.

· • · ● · ● · • ·

Evan and Ava's phones buzzed, and a beep alerted the group that a car was coming up the drive.

"Don't worry," Hank said. "It's Sam. I called him."

Turning to Thomas, he added, "He's the one who can help us. Or Evie. And you, Thomas. Sam is an old friend, used to work for the FBI.

"Sam and his wife, Mira, are part of this group, except now they live in Pittsburgh and run a very successful online food and catering business. But he remains a consultant, and he will know what to do.

"For one thing, there's your frenemy, Ace, Evie. What to do with him? We need Sam to make a deal for him so we can protect him. And then there is your father. How do we stop him, and what does your father do that makes him so dangerous?

"And what about the man that Lex and Johnny have seen? And even though it seems as if this was all about you coming here, Evie, what started it all? That's what I asked myself.

"As Grace asked, 'What are we missing?' And the person who will lead us to the answer is Sam."

Sam heard the last part as he came in the door and said, "No, I think the answer to how this all started lies with your new friend, Thomas Hendrick."

FORTY EIGHT

Duke put on another of his face masks and drove back into Doveland. If anyone was tracking him, he was no longer the man who left his home in the mountains, or even the man who flew into Pittsburgh, where he rented this car.

Knowing where he was going, Duke didn't need a driver. What needed to be done was something he would have to do himself.

He hadn't used so many masks in years. This was another reason he never left home. He hated these masks. But they were a necessary evil, and he was grateful for the man who had made them for him. Of course, that man thought he was making them for a theater production, and Duke never told him otherwise. He had them made years before, and they were not as good as the ones he could have made now. But they were good enough.

As soon as he took care of this business, he would return to being invisible. But first, since he was here anyway, he would put the time to good use. He'd allow himself to relive old memories, even the ones that gave him nightmares. Perhaps it would be a good purging, and it would take care of the headaches that plagued him.

Duke had seen the Diner as he drove around the traffic circle out to the lake. He doubted that it was the same owner, but that it was still there intrigued him, and besides, he was hungry. But first, he would sit in the park. It hadn't been as beautiful when he was a boy. In fact, all of Doveland looked better than what he remembered. It felt better to him, too. He knew no one would know him, even his old classmates.

And even Leo wouldn't know who he was. They had never met. Yet he had been Leo's most significant client for years. And of course, he knew everything about Leo. He couldn't hire a man to physically eliminate his competition, the ones he couldn't convince to sell, or persuade them in other ways to do what he asked, without knowing who he was and what he loved.

With Leo, though, he had been at a disadvantage. Leo had loved his wife, but he still killed her. And Leo loved his daughter as much as could be expected from someone who had no feelings.

Which meant he had to use other means to keep Leo toeing the line since there was no one to threaten him with. But money always worked. The more he paid Leo, the more Leo wanted. And just to be sure, once in a while, Duke gave Leo a little scare, just to remind him who was in charge in case Leo decided to go out on his own or betray him.

Duke sat on the park bench, smiling. He supposed people looking at him might think he was smiling at the beautiful fall day, but instead, he was smiling at the memory of stepping into Leo's mind and tweaking it for a moment.

It was such a kick to take it over and make Leo do something he didn't want to do, like when he had him almost drive off a cliff.

He didn't need to hack a car. He could hack Leo's mind, most anyone's mind, actually. He always stopped in time, but he made sure Leo knew it was him. Those terrifying moments kept Leo loyal.

Yes, he could have tweaked, or hacked, his competitor's minds too, but he chose not to. He chose Leo instead to keep them in line.

If something went wrong, Leo would be caught, not him. They had been in this symbiotic relationship for years. Both of them were pleased with the arrangement.

And then Leo's wife found Leo's diary of jobs. Something so simple made everything go so wrong. Why Leo wrote them down was so stupid he almost eliminated Leo as soon as he heard. Probably he should have. But then Leo took care of the problem.

He chose the work and his personal safety over his wife's life. And stopped keeping records, or so he told him. Now that this had happened, Duke wondered if that was true.

One thing at a time, he told himself.

He had to get what Alice had. Alice had found the diary of her father's jobs that her mother had hidden away for her, and Leo didn't tell him. Duke saw that as a betrayal, but he let Leo try to take care of it himself.

However, since Leo had made the first mistake with his family, Duke had kept track of Alice ever since her mother died. Just in case.

That's how he knew that Alice had found the notebook and tapes years later. He was watching Alice when she tripped on a floorboard after moving the rug covering it to clean the floors.

At first, she didn't know what it was, but her mother had written a note explaining it. Maggie said it was Alice's insurance policy. And when she was ready, Alice was to turn it over to someone who would believe her.

After finding the notebook, Alice had realized that her suspicions about her father were correct. So she left home, and Leo had lost control.

Leo tried to take care of it with Ace. That was useless.

Of course, Ace would fall for Alice, *Duke thought.*

Ace and Alice liking each other made the whole situation worse because it had forced Alice to run. He had tracked her down and hacked into her mind. He intended to have Alice kill herself.

But she blocked him enough, so she didn't die. Instead, she lost her memory. He hadn't done that. Fear of him, and what almost happened, did.

Duke knew that eventually she would remember, and now she had. To make everything worse, Alice was with other people who could block him, which terrified him. And he still didn't know where Alice had put the records.

What made this all so infuriating is that if he had just let it all alone, probably nothing would have come of it. Leo might have been caught. The name he used when he hired Leo was not Duke Quinn. Why had he even bothered?

Looking around the park and then at the Diner, he wondered if it was all because he needed to come back here and deal with the memories. If that was the case, then it worked. Here he was.

But since Leo was here too, he would have to take care of him and the mess he made. Maybe he could use Leo to take care of the chaos, and then he would eliminate him, and he could retreat to his quiet life.

Since he was being honest with himself, Duke knew that as much as he said he loved living by himself and controlling his interests all over the world, and as much as he loved being the puppet master, he was lonely.

He had been lonely his entire life. Controlling people was not the same as being with them.

It felt as if he had swallowed a stone. There it was. The truth. He was lonely. Yes, he was angry. But he knew what to do about the anger. What he didn't know was what to do about the loneliness.

Despite all the people he controlled and all that he owned, he didn't have the one thing that the simplest of people had. Companionship.

Get over yourself, he thought. *You made a choice. It's no one's fault but your own.*

Well, that wasn't entirely true. His life had brought him to that decision. The life that had begun right here in this town. And even though he was sure that no one remembered him, or his mother or father, he remembered. How he had been treated was hard to forget, even though he had tried. Sighing, he stood and walked to the Diner.

Alex watched him through the window. This man was a stranger. He already had a stranger in the Diner. He thought it was odd. And perhaps a bit scary. Pete had always told him to call if he was worried about anything.

When the bell dinged, and the man came in and slid into a booth, Alex took him a menu and asked what he wanted to drink. Then Alex slipped back into the storage room and made the call.

FORTY NINE

"It was a long time ago," Thomas said.

The room stayed silent, waiting for him to fill in the missing pieces.

"I don't see what this has to do with what's going on now. And I've been Thomas Hendrick for so long I barely remember being anyone else."

"But you were someone else," Sam said.

Grace had moved to sit beside Evie on the couch, and Evie had reached over to hold her hand. Her face had gone to the color of snow, making her eyes and hair even more prominent.

She had felt a little guilt at keeping her new name, but it seemed name changing ran in the family.

"Am I really your granddaughter?"

"Yes, you are really my granddaughter," Thomas answered. "My wife, your mother, and you are the best parts of my life. Of course, I haven't had much time with any of you.

"Ann died, Maggie ran away, and I didn't know you existed. There is nothing I would do to harm any of you. And I will do anything to keep you safe and in my life. Changing my name had nothing to do with what's going on."

"But you taught Maggie remote-viewing. Where did you learn it? And why did it take you so long to tell us you did it?" Grace asked.

"First, I didn't realize that you all are aware of it and that even some of you can do it. You don't run around telling people this kind of thing, do you? And second, because I don't anymore.

"I stopped years ago after Maggie ran away because it scared her. She wanted nothing to do with it. I tried to find her by using it, but when I couldn't, I stopped altogether, hating it because it drove Maggie away.

"Over time, it faded the same way my old name did. I suppose I might have started up again if I would have known about all of you. It's my fault. If I would have come out and lived in the community, I suppose I would have learned about all of you and the other "magical" things you do. But I didn't. And I am not sure I can even do remote viewing anymore."

"Somehow, this all goes together," Grace said. "So, who are you?"

"I am Thomas Hendrick. The boy who had another name vanished years ago. My parents worked in some government program, and once it was over, they changed their name and mine. And that's the only reason I have a different name than I was born with. I asked them a few times why we changed our names, and they said it didn't matter. As I got older, I never cared enough to pursue it."

"He's right. The name change doesn't matter. That he is related to the man chasing you does, Evie." Sam said.

"My father?"

"No, the one he works for." Sam paused. "You know what your father does for a living, right?"

Evie nodded. "That's why he wants me. He wants me to turn over the information my mother hid from him, and I found."

"Yes, and so does Duke Quinn."

"As in Quinn Enterprises?"

"That's the one."

"But why him?" Hank asked. "He runs that company behind the scenes. No one knows him. And besides, he is massively successful. What does he have to do with any of this?"

"Everything," Sam answered. "Duke is Leo's biggest client. Duke's name, or one of his aliases, is in the information you have, Evie. If it can be proven that he hires assassins, like your father, to eliminate the competition, it will ruin him. And what you have will go a long way towards that objective."

"Wait," Thomas said. "Did you say I am related to Duke Quinn?"

"Which means I am too?" Evie asked.

"Not related that way," Sam said, and then Evan's phone rang.

$$\bullet \; \bullet \; \bullet \; \bullet \bullet \; \bullet \; \bullet \; \bullet \; \bullet \; \bullet$$

"Stay up here," Pete said to Barbara.

"Not on your life," was her answer as she slipped on her apron and headed downstairs to the Diner.

Once again, she was thankful that their work was right below them. Like Grace, who lived above her coffee shop, they had renovated the floor above the Diner, and now it was home. She loved it. It was just big enough for each of them to have space of their own, and not so big that it required a lot of work to maintain.

Alex said he needed help in the Diner. She was going to help. She glanced behind her at Pete and smiled at him. He couldn't help but smile back at her.

He should have known that if something was going on, she would be in the middle of it. Barbara was an expert at making their customers feel welcome and getting information from them without being intrusive. So if Alex was right and something was going on in the Diner, Barbara would know right away.

Barbara went straight to the coffeepot and started filling coffee cups, welcoming everyone, calling them by name, so by the time she made it to the two strangers, Barbara had established that she was a friendly person.

But neither of them smiled at her or responded beyond a mumble that, yes, they would like more coffee. That's when she turned to Pete and Alex cooking behind the counter and winked at them.

It was Alex who went back into the storage room and made the call.

If Barbara said there was something wrong, then there was.

FIFTY

Thomas stood. "I'll go."

James stood with him. "So will I."

"No," Sam said. "It's too dangerous."

"No, what is too dangerous is storming in there, but we won't do that. It will just be the two of us. Two men sitting at the Diner, having lunch together."

"And what do you hope to accomplish?" Sam asked.

"And they will know who you are," Evie added.

"Does it matter? If one of them recognizes us, we'll go over and talk to them. It's a public place. What could go wrong?"

"Well, so much could go wrong, I can't begin to list it," Sam said. "But the question is, what do you hope to accomplish? Do you think you going to the Diner will stop them?"

"Well, in the long run, probably not. But perhaps we could learn something. And as I said, what's the danger? Besides, do you really know for sure that the two men are Duke and Leo? And do you know for sure Duke is after Leo?" Thomas asked.

"Oh, you are all so ridiculous!" Evie shouted. "It's me who has to go. It's my father. I know he's here.

"I'll go to him and tell him I'm sorry for all the trouble I've caused. He's my father, after all. He must have some love for me."

205

"Even though he sent Ace after you?"

"Yes, especially that. All Ace did was try to find out where I hid the information. He could have done so much more than that, but he didn't."

"Do you have the information?"

"I don't anymore."

Grace laughed, "I think I have to ask again, what are we missing?"

"It's because I have what Leo is after," Sam said. "Well, not me. On the way here, I checked in with my friends at the bureau and asked if they have anything on either of those two men. Not surprisingly, there has been an ongoing investigation for years, but nothing has come of it.

"Except, last month they received information that is proving to be helpful. It was sent to them by an anonymous source, but my guess is that someone in this room sent it to them."

"Yes, it was me," Evie said. "But I hadn't remembered that I had done that. I thought I still had it. However, when I saw Leo, I remembered what I had done. I should have stood up to him then instead of running. I'm tired of running.

"Now, I'll tell him what I did with it loud enough so that this Duke person hears it. As you said, it's a public place. He will not give himself away. Maybe at that point, both of them will start running, and all of you will be safe."

When Sam said nothing, it was Hank who figured it out.

"It's not enough, is it? They would have arrested Duke and Leo before this if you had enough information and proof."

"You want me to wear a wire, don't you?" Evie realized.

"No," Thomas, James, and Owen said at the same time.

Evie smiled at them and turned to Johnny. "You can see and and hear what's going on, can't you without me wearing a wire?"

He nodded.

"Leo and Duke will suspect that I am, so I can't. Have Johnny watch and ask someone in the Diner to turn on their phone. Don't tell me who. You can record it that way. But I can't know anything about it.

"Although I realize I have been blocking someone, I assume it's Duke, I have to let him in enough, so that he won't think I know who he is. Which means the less I know, the better."

"I don't like it," Thomas said.

But Evie had already grabbed James' car keys and was out the door. She was tired of it all. It was time to put a stop to this.

She had wanted to confront her father for years. Today was the day she was going to do it, and at the same time protect her friends. Maybe even have the chance to start a new life.

Briefly, she wondered what Sam meant when he said that she and her grandfather were related somehow to Duke Quinn. But there was no time to worry about that now. First, she had to do the thing she had wanted to do since she first realized that her nightmares were real.

Her father had killed her mother. She was tired of playing nicey-nice. If everyone in the Diner heard her, so much the better.

• • • ● • ● • • • •

Duke drank his coffee, contemplating his next move. Leo's daughter was on the way to the Diner. That he had seen that brief flash of information made him suspicious. He should go. Get Leo later. But he was curious. There was a drama about to be played out, and it might be to his benefit to watch it.

Somehow the woman had made sure that there was no one left in the Diner except him and Leo. It had been subtle and effective.

Duke had seen the young man make the two phone calls. One to bring the owners and one to someone else.

That someone must have told Alice that her father was at the Diner. How many someone else's were involved, Duke didn't know. He thought he would stay a little longer and see what happened since he felt no immediate danger to himself.

Leo, engrossed in his food, hadn't noticed. Duke wondered how he had ever thought that Leo was competent. Well, Leo was an expert at hiring others to do the dirty work, and quite good at the subtle art of eliminating someone when that was necessary.

Which, as Duke thought about it, meant that perhaps Leo wasn't being as unaware as he was pretending to be. Maybe Leo had figured out who he was and was now trying to figure out a way to get out of the whole thing. Which, knowing Leo, would come up with a discreet way to kill him.

Duke glanced at his food. Had it come anywhere near Leo? No, he decided, it hadn't. Safe for now. Leo wasn't safe because he didn't know his daughter was on the way.

Yes, Duke thought, as he took a bite of his sandwich, this was going to be quite a show to watch.

The bell over the door tingled. Duke didn't look up. He knew who it was. Leo didn't bother to look up either because he was busy doing exactly what Duke suspected. He was trying to figure out how to get rid of the man sitting in the other booth.

Yes, he had figured out that it had to be Duke Quinn. And obviously, the people in the Diner knew who they both were and had done an excellent job of making sure they were the only ones left eating.

Yes, he thought, *I will eliminate my best client, but maybe it's time to retire.*

As he ate, Leo thought of all the ways he knew to kill someone and make it look like an accident or a health issue. But all the methods required planning, and he didn't have much time.

Lost in thought, Leo missed the woman until she slid into the booth opposite him.

"Well," he said, not missing a beat, "You came to me."

"Yes," Evie said. "And I came to stop you."

Leo put his hamburger down, picked up his napkin, wiped his face, and then laughed.

"Ah, you have always been a brave, if stupid, girl. How do you expect to do that?"

Evie leaned out of the booth and said to the man in the next one.

"Mr. Quinn, would you like to join us?"

In the park, Johnny said, "No, no, no!" and started to rise.

Sam stopped him. "Let it play out."

FIFTY ONE

Although Sam had tried to stop him, Hank insisted that he go with Johnny and Sam to the park. He would wait in his truck, he said, but there was no way he would not be part of what happened next. Hank and Sam had worked together in the past, and Sam knew he couldn't stop him, so he finally agreed.

That left the men that Evie now called her family—Thomas, James, and Owen—pacing the floor while Valerie and Grace held hands on the couch. They had been through times like this before, but it didn't make it any easier.

Craig remained with Ace and watched the group through the open door of the bedroom. He would have gone with Johnny too, but Johnny had assured him he would be fine, and Ace needed him. Even though he was only Johnny's step-father, Craig loved Johnny and Lex as if they were his own. So although he looked calm, inside his stomach was in knots.

Ava and Evan were in the kitchen making coffee just to have something to do.

Finally, Grace stood up and gestured to the dining room table and said, "Sit, everyone. We are still missing something, so let's figure it out. Craig, put the baby monitor in with Ace and join us."

Once everyone was seated, Grace addressed Thomas.

"Tommy, you seem to be at the center of this. Your daughter, Maggie, ran away. Then she didn't come back because she was trying to protect you from her husband. Why was that? And you said you taught Maggie remote-viewing? Is that part of what is going on? Best you tell us all now. What have you been hiding?"

As Grace addressed Thomas, everyone could see his discomfort. His hands were clenched on the table. A rivet of sweat made its way down the side of his neck.

Across from Thomas, James could feel anger building up inside of him. The urge was so strong to get up and slap Thomas that James had to hold on to his coffee cup for dear life. That this person he was beginning to see as a friend could be the one responsible for the trouble Evie had been in made him tremble with rage.

James thought he had defeated that part of himself. It had shown up in his marriage and destroyed it. Feeling it again scared him.

Breathing deeply, he shut his eyes and calmed himself the best that he could, hoping that what Thomas said wouldn't destroy Evie's life, or make him hate the man.

Thomas took out a handkerchief and wiped his face before saying, "I didn't know."

Grace sighed and put her hand on Thomas' arm.

"Talk. We'll listen. If you're at fault, we will still listen and help you. But unless you help us fill in the missing pieces, your granddaughter is still in danger. And even though none of us know you well, we know that you love her."

Thomas nodded. "Love her. Love Maggie and my wife, Ann. I never meant to put any of them in danger, and until all of this happened, I didn't realize that I had."

Looking around the room, Thomas' voice trembled as he said, "You have to believe me. I didn't do any of this on purpose."

It was Ava who spoke this time.

"I've done some amazingly stupid things in my life, Tommy. And this group of people helped me uncover my past and forgive myself for it. But that only happened after I let them help me. So let us help you now. What are we missing?"

Thomas sighed. "I'm not sure how it all ties in. Perhaps you all can see it better because you are not in the middle of it. Because as you know, when you live inside something, you can't see the big picture. And that's what I was working on at my job. Seeing outside of what the five senses think is the limit to how life exists. And the company that had hired me to do that was Quinn Enterprises."

When Evan started to say something, Thomas held up his hand.

"No. I never met the man. Who has? Besides, it was a subsidiary, and until this all began, I hadn't stopped to think about who owned it. But it is a missing piece, isn't it? And now I think I understand why I was let go so abruptly, and why they completely shut me out afterward."

"What were you working on?" James asked, the grip on his coffee cup getting lighter.

"Portals to other dimensions. I know it sounds like a fantasy, but it's a possibility that it could be done."

Except for James and Owen, everyone else didn't look surprised. Ava and Evan exchanged glances, and Grace looked down at her hands.

"Not news to you?" Thomas asked.

"No. But that's for another time," Grace said. "Still, what does that have to do with your daughter protecting you and Duke Quinn being here."

"I think they fired me because I was so close to figuring out how we could do it. Perhaps Duke wanted to keep that a secret for himself? Why, I don't know. Even so, why get rid of me?"

"Still missing a sizable piece of information here," Grace said. "You said your parents worked for the government and then changed their names. Given what we know based on our experiences in the past, I assume that they were remote viewers, which is why you have that gift?"

"They were, even though it was a subject we mostly ignored. It was very hush-hush. But the few times we talked about it got me interested in other dimensions and energy fields in this dimension. The ability to remote view was one thing. What else was there? That's what I wanted to know."

Grace paused, trying to get her thoughts in order.

"So Duke Enterprises hired you to find a portal. You almost did. You got fired, or let go, which may or may not have something to do with why your daughter felt she had to protect you. Did she not want her husband to know what you could do?

"It doesn't make sense, you know, since you weren't the only one studying this, and many people can remote view or read minds, and even yes, some move between dimensions.

"Stopping you wouldn't have stopped them. However, we have experienced people trying to stop this kind of information from becoming public. Is that what this is all about?"

"No, not just that," Ace said, standing in the doorway gripping the door frame with both hands.

"It's about your wife."

FIFTY TWO

"**M**an, I thought I was a better fighter than that," Ace said as Craig lowered him into a chair.

Most of what had happened to Ace wasn't visible, but his face was ashen, and his eyes were bloodshot. He was wearing one of Evan's sweatshirts because Craig had to cut off the shirt he was wearing to bandage his ribs.

Owen squinted his eyes at him, reserving judgment. This was one of the men Ava had been running away from, but then he had come to her rescue, so he felt that he should also be grateful for him.

Ace did his best to smile at Owen, recognizing his confusion.

"I'm confused too. I never intended to care about Alice..."

"Evie, her name is Evie," Owen broke in.

"Okay, if you say so. Evie. I was in debt to Leo. I thought it would be a simple job. Then it wasn't. And once she went missing, I realized how much I cared about her, and I wanted to find her before her father did."

He dropped his head and mumbled, "I guess my timing was a little off."

"It was good enough, dear," Grace said. "But that doesn't matter right now. We need to find out what is going on so we can keep her

214

and our friends safe. What did you mean when you said that it is about Thomas' wife?"

"Sorry, man," Ace said, looking at Thomas. "You will not like this. And I only know about it because I overheard a phone call between Leo and Duke Quinn. I didn't put it together until you said the name Ann a minute ago. So I figure it has to be connected."

"But you don't know how?" Grace asked, keeping her hand on Thomas' arm. She could feel the tremor running through his body, waiting to hear what Ace was going to say.

"Not for sure, but it makes sense. I hope. I don't want to make more trouble. I really just want to help."

"What did you hear, Ace?" Craig asked. He had his hand on Ace's shoulder, hoping that it would calm him.

Ace paused before answering.

"Leo said, 'You knew Maggie's mother, Ann?'

"And then he started yelling about it, but went into another room, so I didn't hear more. All I know is that from that point on, finding Alice, I mean Evie, was priority number one for Leo. I wasn't supposed to hurt her, just find the information and get it and her back to Leo. He said he would take it from there."

Nobody said anything until Owen blurted out.

"That's it? How can that mean anything?"

This time it was Valerie who answered him. She remembered what had happened when she discovered that her husband, Harold, had deep connections with the man who had been both the town's doctor and the town's serial killer.

Sometimes, it was the small things that revealed the entire picture. It was Harold's death that had finally opened everyone's eyes to the truth about the town's doctor. He had been a man everyone in town had loved.

Valerie knew that sometimes what seemed like a minor connection brought the entire picture into focus.

"I think the question is, how did Ann know Duke? And how well."

Thomas stood, knocking down his chair, his hands clenched so hard that Grace could see the imprint of his fingernails in the palms of his hand.

"No. It can't be about Ann. No!"

James righted Thomas' chair, and Grace took his hand and pulled him back down.

"But if it is, don't you want to know? Wouldn't Ann want Evie to be safe, the same way that you do?"

Thomas' head dropped, and he whispered, "Yes."

"Okay," Grace said. "This seems to be my favorite thing to say about what is going on: What are we missing? How would Ann have known Duke, and why does that matter now?"

· · · ● ●· ● ● · ·

Leo stared at his daughter in horror as she asked the man behind them to join them. And she called him Mr. Quinn? How did she know?

Inside, he groaned and thought about how he was going to get out of this. Behind him, he heard a familiar laugh and realized Alice was right. It was Duke Quinn. He had heard that laugh enough times to have it engraved in his soul. If he had one.

It wasn't a pleasant laugh. If someone designed an evil doll with a sinister laugh, that was what it would sound like. It had always sent a frisson of fear down his spine when he heard it over the phone. And now that it was only a few feet behind him, it raised goosebumps on his arms, and it felt as if the hair on the back of his neck had stood up. He had read about such things but never experienced them before. Yes, it was true. He was terrified.

"What are you doing?" he hissed at his daughter.

"Settling this," she answered back.

Duke had risen and brought a chair to the table. There was no way he was going to sit beside the bumbling idiot and across from a girl who thought she could interrogate him. He was in charge. He had always been in charge. Everyone needed to know that, including Ann's granddaughter.

It annoyed him to no end that he couldn't get into that girl's mind either. Was the ability to block other people's thought a gift or a learned practice?

He heard the echo of Ann's words, "It's both, Luke."

And at that moment, in the Diner, Duke's past came rushing back. The one he thought he had left behind.

But that girl, that girl looking at him now, could have been his Ann. He had made the wrong choice in the past. What choice would he make now?

FIFTY THREE

Luke, what a name, Duke thought. He assumed his mother liked the name and thought it would make him brave and good, like the Luke in the Bible. That was what he imagined.

Maybe his stupid father named him that, but he doubted it. What did his father know about the Bible?

He had vague memories of sitting on his mother's lap while she read the Bible to him. That was before she got sick and died. Before he was alone and stuck with his abusive father. Before he found the tool he used to control his father, and then all the people around him—with a few significant and dangerous exceptions.

Like this girl, and now the people she had collected who were determined to help her.

If only she didn't look like Ann. But she did. Exactly like her. The same bright blue eyes and flaming hair. But Ann always looked at him with love, and this girl looked at him with contempt. No fear. Just contempt.

If things had gone the way he wanted them to, this girl could have been his granddaughter. Perhaps then she would look at him with love the same way that Ann had.

But no. Thomas Hendrick had taken Ann, and now her granddaughter, away from him.

Duke stayed silent, waiting for who would speak first. But Alice also remained silent, waiting for him, and Leo was too shocked to say anything.

What if I explain how I felt? Duke wondered. Would it change anything?

How it felt to have a name like Luke Sharpe. How my mother never knew how mean boys could be. How they taunted me, calling me "Look sharp, lukie dukie."

It was only words, but they cut deep. He had loved the name Luke, and they ruined it. Then they started using fists and feet to subdue him instead of just words. Small for his age, he was easy prey until he discovered his power to defeat them with his mind.

Through all that, there was one girl in school who stood up for him. She treated him with kindness. At first, he had been mean to her, then one day, she stood up to him and said, "Stop."

It was his word. The one he used to stop his father and the bullies, and it took him by surprise.

"Stop what?"

"Stop trying to make me hate you."

"Is that what I am doing?"

"It is. You can't make me. You can't turn me into a mean person. You can't tell me what to do. I choose to like you."

At twelve, Ann was a few inches taller than him. By the time they were eighteen, he was a foot taller than her, but that day, she leaned down and poked him in the chest.

"Somewhere inside of you is a good heart. I know you want to kill it. I hope you won't. Still, I won't let you kill mine."

No matter what he did for the next six years, Ann still smiled at him. But when he said he was leaving town and asked her to go with him, that's when she killed his heart for good.

It had been missing ever since.

BECA LEWIS

She said no. She would be his friend, but she couldn't live the life that he planned to live. She was going to college, and she would study quantum mechanics.

"But girls don't do that," he had said with a sneer.

"Well, this girl does," she smiled back, and then flicked a strand of hair back from her eyes. He had loved the gesture, but that time it told him he had lost her for good.

That day, he had barely contained the rage he felt. His one friend was going to abandon him. Now all he had left was his power to control other people, even if he couldn't control her.

As always, Ann read what he was thinking. She had a gift. Not just the gifts of equanimity and kindness combined with a searing intelligence. She had the same gift that he had. She just didn't use it like him. She controlled it. Discovering that she could read minds, sometimes, and that people responded to her wishes, she wanted to know why.

She realized early that using her gifts for bad would only destroy her in the end. She tried to tell Luke that too. She tried to save him. He refused.

That day she tried one more time.

"I am not abandoning you, Luke. I am trying to show you another way."

"Without me!" he shouted.

"Without you until you stop using your gifts for evil. You get to choose."

"It's too late," Luke had whispered, and walked away.

He changed his name that day to Duke Quinn. Duke, because it was like Luke. Quinn, because Ann loved the way the letter q looked when she wrote it. Sometimes she had called herself Annie Q.

He left town that day and purposively never tried to find her again. He knew she understood why. He couldn't be part of her life, and he didn't want to know what he had missed.

220

And then, one day, almost fifty years later, after a long successful, but lonely life, he found something that changed everything.

He owned so many companies that he couldn't, and didn't, pay much attention to what they were doing unless they were losing money.

But he had an open search for what was happening in quantum mechanics and quantum physics. It was his one connection to his past. It was his silent homage to Ann. In fact, he was often an anonymous donor to studies about things like remote-viewing, mind reading, and teleportation.

He even owned a company that researched how to open portals into other dimensions. He thought it would be a great way to escape if he had to. Open a portal, and poof, he was gone. Maybe live another life, start over. Perhaps find Ann there.

Duke didn't actually believe it. But it sounded interesting. It gave him a purpose and filled some of the lonely spaces in his life.

Then one day, he read about a man named Thomas Hendrick who was studying the possibilities of portals.

So what, he had thought to himself. And then he read Thomas' bio. Thomas had been married to a woman named Ann.

At that moment, his world collapsed on itself. Months passed before he could think about it again. Ann had died, but she had a daughter named Maggie.

That's when everything clicked into place for Duke. The universe had brought Ann back to him. How it happened didn't matter. But the man he had hired to take care of his problem people had been married to Ann's daughter, Maggie.

Except, Maggie had died too, years before in an accident. And although he couldn't prove it, Duke knew that Leo had killed her. It was his style. From that moment on, Duke was determined to punish Leo. He would wait for the perfect moment to confront him, but Duke knew that one day he would have the chance to take his revenge.

In the meantime, he had one more chance. Ann's granddaughter Alice. He found Alice and tried to hire her. She said no, just like her mother, and for the same reason.

And now, here she was in front of him and her father, confronting both of them about their evil ways and planning to turn over the information to the authorities that would take them both down. Even though she was Ann's daughter, he had to stop her before she did.

That's when Alice turned to Duke and said, "I already did."

FIFTY FOUR

I t was the last straw. He had nothing left to lose.

Duke took one last look at the girl who looked exactly like the love of his life, and the man who had killed her daughter, closed his eyes and opened up the full force of his mind.

He directed it towards the two people sitting in front of him and reached out and found the man who had married his Ann and included him in his attack.

At Ava's, Thomas collapsed on the floor, holding his head.

In the Diner, Leo's eyes rolled back in his head, and he fell off his chair.

Out in the park, Johnny ran towards the Diner—Hank, and Sam following close behind.

For a moment, Duke felt as if he was a god. Total power. Everyone in his control. No more hole in his heart. No more missing his Ann. Just the pure pleasure of his focused intent to destroy.

"Stop!" Evie said.

Duke opened his eyes and had the fleeting thought that somehow he had brought Ann back to him.

She was standing above him, just as she had done years before.

"Stop!' She repeated, poking him in the chest in that same way.

Except this wasn't Ann. And with that awareness, all the power he had been projecting collapsed, and his heartfelt as if it was exploding. The heart he thought he had lost years before was still there. But the pain was so intense he couldn't breathe.

Duke blinked again. Now there were two of them. Two women with flaming red hair and bright blue eyes stood above him as he lay on the floor of the Diner.

Behind the women, he could see the sign that said "open." For a moment, he felt as if that was another message from the universe.

Open what? Duke asked himself as he drifted away from the pain.

One of the blue-eyed women smiled at him as the mist closed in. "Luke, why didn't you listen?"

Luke closed his eyes, wondering why he hadn't.

· · · ● · ● · · ·

Johnny, Sam, and Hank burst through the door, almost knocking the bell off its chain. Pete and Barbara were already in action, each one doing CPR. Pete on Duke. Barbara on Leo. Alex was on the phone, calling for an ambulance.

But it wasn't the men that Johnny was concerned about. He rushed towards Evie, who was watching Pete and Barbara work on her father and Duke without moving.

I did this, she thought. *It's my fault. How could I have let this happen? I'm as evil as my father.*

Johnny reached her just in time as her knees bent, and she crumpled to the floor.

This time it was Johnny who said, "Stop," but so quietly that only Evie barely heard him.

"Don't let that inside your head," he whispered. "You know what it can do. Stop it."

Evie looked at Johnny. He nodded, and mind-spoke to her. "Whatever happened here was not your fault. You chose good. They chose evil. Not your fault."

Evie closed her eyes, and Johnny could feel her slipping away.

"Choose to stay, Evie," he said, as firmly as he could. "Your grandfather needs you. And so do James and Owen. And me. Don't leave. Please."

If Johnny had looked behind him, he would have seen two women holding hands and crying, but he was focused only on Evie.

· · · ● · ● · · ·

At Ava's, Thomas had stopped holding his head, but he still lay on the floor, not moving. Craig bent over him.

Everyone in the room held their breath. Grace reached out to hold Valerie's hand. Ace closed his eyes and slumped back into the couch. Owen and James knelt beside Thomas, Owen openly weeping. Until that moment, he hadn't fully realized that he had included Thomas in his family.

"He can't die," Owen whispered.

FIFTY FIVE

"Not my time, kid," Thomas whispered from the floor. "But boy, did that hurt. What was that?"

Craig helped him sit up, and Ava handed him a glass of water while holding her phone to her ear. She said nothing, just listened.

After Craig and Owen got Thomas to the couch with Ace, she told them what she knew.

She looked at two men who used to be on opposite sides of the problem—now on opposite sides of the couch both looking the worse for wear, but both still alive—and thought how it could have been such a different outcome. That was more than could be said for the two that started it.

But instead of telling them that, she told them what they all wanted most to hear—that Evie was a little shaken up but okay. Johnny was with her, and he and Hank were bringing her to Ava's.

"Thank God," Thomas breathed. "I think I would have wanted to die if something happened to her."

Ava chose not to tell them that Evie wasn't strictly okay. Instead, she gestured to Grace to come to the kitchen with her.

"What is it?" Grace asked.

"She needs our help. Johnny asked us to contact Bryan and Rachel and have them meet them here."

Grace knew what that meant. Evie was trying to decide whether to come or go. Bryan had been helping people in the in-between the past few months. Rachel was his grounding, both in life and when he did his work in the in-between.

A few months before, they had helped a woman who had died to go back into her past and correct a mistake she had made. But since it altered the outcome of the woman's life, very few people involved remembered what had happened. It had been Bryan and Rachel who had made it work, which is why Johnny wanted them.

She dialed Bryan's number, and Rachel answered, which made Grace smile. Rachel and Bryan had married a few months before after loving each other since childhood. Their mothers, in the in-between, had brought them together.

"Finally," Jillyan, Bryan's mother, had whispered in Grace's ear at the wedding. Grace hadn't seen Jillyan since then. Bryan said she had left and gone to be with his father.

"We need you and Bryan at Ava's," was all Grace said.

"Five minutes," was Rachel's answer and hung up.

· · · ● ● ● ● ● · ·

At the Diner, Barbara was directing the traffic as best as she could. It was a small Diner, and it was packed with people trying to help.

They had turned the open sign to closed, which is precisely what had happened. A chapter of two men's lives had closed.

Could we have done anything differently? she asked herself.

As an answer to her unspoken question, Johnny had said out loud what he had said to Evie, "They did it to themselves."

As Sam watched, he knew he would have a hard time explaining how two men sitting in chairs had died at the same time. And how one girl was unconscious.

But it was Doveland. The people of Doveland were used to strange things happening in their town. All he had to do was come up with a reasonable explanation, and they would slip the rest under the rug. He hoped.

The mess that would follow, once everyone discovered that one of these men was Duke Quinn from Quinn Enterprises, well that wasn't his problem.

He could go back to Mira and their catering business and their busy but slightly dull life. Just how he liked it. Once the basic questions were answered, he would get out of town as quickly as possible.

One of the EMTs asked if Sam wanted to ride with them, and he said yes. He could pick up his car later. They would go to the hospital first, only to officially declare that the two men had died.

Johnny had told them that Evie had fainted, and he and Hank would take her to Ava's where the town's doctor already was and take care of her there.

The EMTs were happy to oblige. What happened was already going to be a hard thing to explain. One less person would make it easier.

Dan, the police chief, had arrived with the ambulances. He had looked at who was in the Diner and knew that there was a bigger story than what Sam was telling them. After all, Sam was in town. He knew what that meant.

But Dan also knew that the Doveland Karass, as they called themselves now, would take care of it. And if he wanted to know more, Sam would tell him. Dan was not sure he did.

Instead, he shook Sam's hand, nodded at Hank and Johnny as they carried a girl he had never seen before to Hank's truck, accepted a cup of coffee from Pete and a hug from Barbara, and sighed.

It was never boring in Doveland. But he loved it anyway.

FIFTY SIX

Bryan and Rachel pulled into Ava's at the same time as Hank. Bryan could see the girl that Johnny was holding. He knew who she was. He had already met her.

On the way over, he had stepped into the in-between as Rachel drove. Stepping in wasn't the best term for it, but it was the only way he knew how to describe the sensation of entering a different space than the one his physical body lived in.

Although he had resisted the work at first, he had let go of the resistance over the last few months, and now it was easier. That didn't mean that it was always enjoyable, though. Although it had become more comfortable to step in, not everyone wanted his help, or did they become nicer because they had died.

No, people were what they were when they passed on. It made sense to Bryan. They weren't actually dead. Life couldn't die. They just opened the door to go to the next place.

Just opening doors didn't change anyone in this life either, he thought. It takes willingness and awareness. Something he was working on himself.

Not everyone went to the in-between. Some went "straight-through," as he called it. Others lingered. Either because they chose to, or they wouldn't accept that they had died, or needed to complete something first.

Evie was not actually in the in-between because she hadn't walked through the door yet. She was in what he called a decision room. Some people called them near-death-experiences, and he supposed that was an appropriate description.

In-between life and death, but not in-between death and life. It was a distinction that Bryan had only just begun to make and he had only helped one other person in that decision space. He hoped that he knew enough now to help this young woman who was so crucial to friends of his.

Evie was where she was because she was grieving and blaming herself for what happened to her mother, father, and even Duke Quinn.

That's not what she told him when he met her there. Evie said she couldn't go on knowing that her saying "stop" had caused such a horrible result. Who was she to think she had a right to do that?

That's where Bryan had left her, saying he would be back. She hadn't responded other than to mumble, "Okay."

He needed more help, and he hoped that Johnny could provide it. But when Bryan walked into the house, he realized he would get help from two people he had never met. No one else seemed to know that they were there, so he was the one who spoke to them.

Seeing Bryan speak to the air, surprised no one. But when he asked the two women if they would be willing to let others see them and opened up the others' temporary ability to see them—and they did—it was Thomas who started to cry.

"Ann and Maggie," he said, trying to get up from the couch.

"No, stay there," the older woman said. "We can't stay long. We came for Alice."

"You're taking her away?" Johnny cried, still holding Evie.

"No, dear," Ann said, "We came to tell her to stay."

"And meet you, of course," Maggie added. Looking around the room, she said, "All of you. Not just this young man who is such a big part of our girl's future."

Ace, watching people talk to two women who looked like ghosts to him, thought he might have died after all. Dead or crazy, that was the conclusion.

"This can't be happening. Who are you? Did I die?"

Maggie smiled at him, "No. But you made a choice that will allow you to live. We wanted to thank you and remind you that you can stay on this course of doing the right thing. Don't go back."

Turning to Johnny, she asked, "Could you take Evie into the other room? We want to talk privately with her."

As Johnny carried Evie into the other room, the two women turned to Thomas, who remained on the couch with tears running down his face.

Ann sat down beside him, and Maggie knelt in front of him. As they did so, they were no longer visible to anyone in the room except Thomas and Bryan.

"I miss you both so much," Thomas said.

"We know, but you have to live now," Ann said. "Will you do that for us, and Alice?

"Bryan, we would love your help with Leo and Duke. Actually, he is Luke to me," Ann said.

"You want to help them, after who they are and what they did?" Bryan asked.

"This is when they need it the most. If we don't help them now, they are lost in the cycle they created," Ann said. "We both loved these men. That love can save them now, but we will need your help to convince them and then make that transition."

Bryan sighed. He had learned that he couldn't say no. It was a gift that he had been given that had to be used.

"My honor," he bowed.

Turning to Rachel, he said, "Could you drive us to the hospital? Evie will be fine with Johnny and her mother and grandmother."

After a round of hugs and thank yous, Bryan and Rachel were gone, leaving everyone staring at the closed bedroom door where Johnny and Evie had gone.

Sam called not long after that and told them they had declared both men DOA. It looked as if Leo had died of a massive heart attack and Duke from a burst aneurysm. The authorities were leaning towards calling it a freak coincidence, and no one would, or could, tell them otherwise.

There would be a massive fallout from Evie's information, and it would take years before they would sort out Quinn Enterprises. But none of that would affect the people of Doveland, so for them, the story was over.

But the people waiting at Ava's for Evie to decide knew that story hadn't been told yet. So they did what they knew how to do.

They sat together quietly, letting the love they felt for each other fill the space. Ace, not understanding what they were doing, found that when he closed his eyes he could feel, maybe for the first time in his life, what love felt like. He discovered that it was what he wanted to move toward. They had given him a second chance to grab what he had been missing, and he was going to take it.

Inside the closed room, Johnny, Ann, and Maggie spoke with Alice, newly named Evie, and hoped that what they had to say brought her back to the life that was waiting for her.

FIFTY SEVEN

If anyone had looked in the room, they would have seen Evie lying on the bed, her head resting on Johnny's shoulder. Both looked like they were sleeping. But they weren't.

They were with Ann and Maggie.

Evie and Johnny were sitting in separate chairs while the two women stood before them.

"You and Evie look so much alike," Johnny said to Ann.

Ann beamed with pleasure and reached out to hold Maggie's hand.

"She has her mother's adventurous spirit, though."

"I want to go with you two," Evie cried. "Mom, I've been so lonely without you. I miss you so much! And I never got to meet my grandmother. I see you now, but I don't know you. It's not fair. And it's not fair that my father took you away from me."

"But Evie," Maggie said. "Look at me. That's not the right choice. You'd be running away.

"You would never choose to do that, would you? There is an entire life for you to live before you. People to love. Adventure. And you no longer need to hide.

"Your grandmother and I want you to live a life that neither of us had time to live. You have people that love you already. It would devastate your grandfather. He just met you, and then you die on him too? You can't do that to him, Evie. You have to choose to live. Fully. Without regret."

"But I killed my father and that Duke guy. I can't live with that."

"By saying 'stop?'" Ann said. "You said that to Luke the same way that I did when we were eighteen. I didn't kill him then, and you didn't kill him now.

"He chose to use his gifts for evil. You said stop to it, and it stopped him. That it killed him was because the evil he had been doing turned on him as it always will. You didn't kill him or your father. They did that to themselves.

"If Luke would have listened to me when we were young, he could have lived a satisfying life. He would not have needed to change his name. He could have used his gift for good. I would have stayed in his life.

"No, we still wouldn't have married, even though he thought we would. He was my friend, and I was there for him. But it was Thomas that I was meant to marry, and I don't regret a moment of it.

"You can't let regret and false guilt steal your life away, Evie," Maggie said.

By then, Evie was openly crying, and Johnny had to force himself to let her.

Maggie smiled at him, and he knew he was making the right choice to let Evie find her way on her own.

"Evie," Ann said. "Would it help to talk to Leo and Luke?"

"Can I?" Evie said, looking up at her grandmother.

Turning to Johnny, Ann said, "We won't see you again, Johnny, but thank you for taking care of our girl."

Johnny smiled, nodded, and then found himself back on the bed, with Evie's head on his shoulder. He'd wait until she finished doing what she needed to do, but he was no longer afraid. Because now he knew she would come back.

FIFTY EIGHT

Thomas held the Christmas party at his house. He had never hosted a Christmas party before. He and Ann had always celebrated Christmas together. Just the two of them. They would get an enormous tree and decorate it together.

Both of them would wrap presents for each other and put them under the tree. They'd stare at that tree every day, waiting for the moment they could unwrap their gifts together.

Then Ann was gone, and it was just him and Maggie, and he tried to recreate the magic he and Ann had shared. He tried to imagine what Ann would have done if she was still there and experience it as if it was still the three of them together. Sometimes it worked. He could almost feel Ann beside him.

His favorite part of Christmas with Maggie was Christmas morning. Christmas Eve, they would open one present apiece, and then he would tuck her into bed and give her two butterfly kisses. One from her mother and one from him. Once Maggie went to sleep, he would get all the presents he had been hiding all year in the attic and put them around the tree.

When Maggie came out of her room in the morning, he'd be waiting for her, no matter what time it was, because he never went to bed. He never wanted to miss seeing her face light up at the tree blinking on and off and stacks of presents waiting for her.

He'd make her a special breakfast, and then they would spend the rest of the day watching movies and overeating.

When Maggie got older, she wasn't interested in spending the entire day with him, and he found it harder and harder to get her face to light up.

During all these years, he had not allowed himself to admit how much he had missed it.

But now, he had it again. Because even though Evie was a grown up woman in her eyes, he had treated her to a Christmas just like the ones he had experienced with Ann and then Maggie. And Evie had loved it. She, too, had been missing the Christmas mornings that her mother had given her before she died.

Evie and Thomas had laughed and cried together, no longer missing anything at all.

Both of them had said goodbye to Ann and Maggie, without regret. They understood that it was time for Ann and Maggie to move on, and they'd find each other again.

As Grace had said to them at Leo's funeral, people find each other again in every lifetime.

"But we have to fully live the one we have," Grace had said. "Otherwise, we miss why we are here."

Evie figured Grace would know. In the past few months, she had gotten to know the members of the Doveland Karass better and heard many of their stories. All fascinating. She would miss them.

She had decided to go back to school, and James and Owen were going with her. Owen was going to school too. She only had a few years left, but he was just beginning. They would help each other.

James had made all the arrangements. She called him dad now. At first, she worried that her grandfather would feel bad about her decision to make James and Owen family. But he had assured her she had chosen good men for a dad and a brother.

Besides, he would always be her grandfather, and all three of them would come to visit over the holidays. He had friends now, he assured her. He would be okay.

Even Ace, before being whisked off into the witness protection program, had told her she was doing the right thing.

"You'll find someone special," she had whispered to him.

They had stood together for a moment, foreheads touching, letting go. Then Ace smiled and walked away. She had told him "thank you" enough times that she hoped he believed it.

In the hospital, it had been the same with her father. Although he and Duke had died in the Diner, they were both still in the in-between.

Evie had thanked Leo for the things he had done for her. She forgave him for what he hadn't done and told him he now had another choice. She hoped he would make a better one this time.

The man she knew as Duke had stared at her a long time until he said, "I should have listened to your grandmother. By not listening, I missed everything good about life, thinking that I wasn't missing anything by controlling things. I was a fool."

"I'm sorry," she said.

"Nothing to be sorry about," he said. "I'm the one who should say, I'm sorry. But let me just warn you, I will still be watching you."

Evie had gasped and stepped back, and Duke laughed. "Not that way, kid. Watching you make a good life for yourself."

Ann had stretched out her hand, and Duke had taken it. Leo had taken Maggie's, and Evie had returned to Ava's house to find herself being watched over by the one person she would miss the most when she left Doveland.

Looking across the room at him now, with the tree lights and the candles and the festive wreaths circling the living room, Evie smiled at him. Johnny had told her to go too. He had to finish school, and so did she.

Doveland would be their home base. Just because they were missing each other didn't mean that they weren't together. That's how he saw it, and now she did too.

So when everyone piled into Thomas' house for Christmas dinner, there were no regrets about decisions made. Only joy at anticipating what the new year would bring.

THE END

Author's Note

After writing the book that comes before this one—- *In-Between*—I realized how much I missed Doveland and the people who live there.

So I decided to stay awhile and see who else wanted to be part of the Doveland community. As a result, a girl named Evie showed up and told me her story.

I had taken a couple of years away from Doveland to write two spin-off series. In them, a few people who had been part of the Forest and Stone Circles have gone off to other dimensions (Erda) and planets (Thamon).

I thoroughly enjoy making up whole new worlds, but Doveland is like home. It was time to come back and see what everyone was up to, and after returning, it was easy to stay for a while.

In *Missing*, I wanted to explore how many ways we allow what is important to go missing, either through our own choices, or because we feel they were taken from us.

However, although people, places, and things may appear to be missing, we can never lose the true essence of Life. Knowing this to be true gives us hope that all is well.

Hope, based on the understanding that love is the only power; possibilities, community, and action are the backbone of Doveland and why I love it there.

Sometimes, as I write Doveland stories, I walk the streets in my mind, and it is as real as the towns I have lived in and loved. Doveland is a combination of a few of them, taking the best from each. It's a walking town, and I love a walking town. Even if I don't live in one now physically, I do in my imagination.

I hope Doveland feels like home to you, too, and we can meet in the Diner, or Your Second Home, or Ava's or Grace's, and have a chat one day.

Yes, there will be more stories from Doveland. There will always be another person or two who finds Doveland and brings an adventure to the people that live there. It's quite exciting for me to see who turns up, and I hope that it is for you, too. —Beca

PS

Thank you for reading my books. Otherwise, it would just be me and the words, and although words are lovely, it's the sharing of them that makes it all worthwhile. Thank you for reading and sharing mine.

You can find all of my books at your favorite book store or on my website: becalewis.com

· · · ● ● ● · ● · · ·

CONNECT WITH ME ONLINE:

Facebook: https://www.facebook.com/becalewiscreative
Facebook: https://www.facebook.com/becalewisfans
Instagram: https://instagram.com/becalewis
TikTok: https://tiktok.com/@becalewis
Twitter: http://twitter.com/becalewis
LinkedIn: https://linkedin.com/in/becalewis
Youtube: https://www.youtube.com/c/becalewis

ACKNOWLEDGEMENTS

I could never write a book without the help of my friends and my book community. Thank you, Jet Tucker, Jamie Lewis, Diana Cormier, and Barbara Budan for taking the time to do the final reader proof. You are a loyal and much-loved reader team. You can't imagine how much I appreciate it.

A huge thank you to Laura Moliter for her fantastic book editing.

Thank you to every other member of my Book Community who helps me make so many decisions that help the book be the best book possible.

Thank you to all the people who tell me that they love to read these stories. Those random comments from friends and strangers are more valuable than gold.

And as always, thank you to my beloved husband, Del, for being my daily sounding board, for putting up with all my questions, my constant need to want to make things better, and for being the love of my life, in more than just this one lifetime.

ALSO BY BECA

The Ruby Sisters Series: Women's Lit, Friendship
A Last Gift, After All This Time, ...
Stories From Doveland: Magical Realism, Friendship
Karass, Pragma, Jatismar, Exousia, Stemma, Paragnosis,
In-Between, Missing, Out Of Nowhere
The Return To Erda Series: Fantasy
Shatterskin, Deadsweep, Abbadon, The Experiment
The Chronicles of Thamon: Fantasy
Banished, Betrayed, Discovered, Wren's Story
The Shift Series: Spiritual Self-Help
Living in Grace: The Shift to Spiritual Perception
The Daily Shift: Daily Lessons From Love To Money
The 4 Essential Questions: Choosing Spiritually Healthy Habits
The 28 Day Shift To Wealth: A Daily Prosperity Plan
The Intent Course: Say Yes To What Moves You
Imagination Mastery: A Workbook For Shifting Your Reality
Right Thinking: A Thoughtful System for Healing
Perception Mastery: Seven Steps To Lasting Change
Perception Parables: Very short stories
Love's Silent Sweet Secret: A Fable About Love
Golden Chains And Silver Cords: A Fable About Letting Go

Advice:
A Woman's ABC's of Life: Lessons in Love, Life, and Career from Those Who Learned The Hard Way

About Beca

Beca writes books she hopes will change people's perceptions of themselves and the world, and open possibilities to things and ideas that are waiting to be seen and experienced.

At sixteen, Beca founded her own dance studio. Later, she received a Master's Degree in Dance in Choreography from UCLA and founded the Harbinger Dance Theatre, a multimedia dance company, while continuing to run her dance school.

After graduating—to better support her three children—Beca switched to the sales field, where she worked as an employee and independent contractor to many industries, excelling in each while perfecting and teaching her Shift® system, and writing books.

She joined the financial industry in 1983 and became an Associate Vice President of Investments at a major stock brokerage firm, and was a licensed Certified Financial Planner for over twenty years.

This diversity, along with a variety of life challenges, helped fuel the desire to share what she's learned by writing and speaking, hoping it will make a difference in other people's lives.

Beca grew up in State College, PA, with the dream of becoming a dancer and then a writer. She carried that dream forward as she fulfilled a childhood wish by moving to Southern California in 1968. Beca told her family she would never move back to the cold.

After living there for thirty-one years, she met her husband Delbert Lee Piper, Sr., at a retreat in Virginia, and everything changed. They decided to find a place they could call their own, which sent them off traveling around the United States. They lived and worked in a few different places before returning to live in the cold once again near Del's family in a small town in Northeast Ohio, not too far from State College.

When not working and teaching together, they love to visit and play with their combined family of eight children and five grandchildren, read, study, do yoga or taiji, feed birds, and work in their garden.

Made in the USA
Coppell, TX
21 April 2022